Tears for
a tall horse

Ann Wigley

Tears for
a tall horse

Chapter One

I found it very difficult to come to terms with the fact that my father had left us for good. He simply walked away to start a new life with a new wife and family in another country, leaving my Mom and me to pick up the pieces as best we could. I knew that divorce happened in lots of families, but that did not make it any easier to bear. I managed to cope only because I had such a wonderful relationship with my mother. I was an only child and we had always been very close, more like sisters than mother and daughter.

To make matters worse, we lost our home as well. Dad had worked at Swayle Farm, Swallowbridge, where we lived in a tied cottage that went with his job. Mr. Swayle was very kind and let Mom and me stay in the cottage for several months, but he needed it for the new stockman. Eventually we had to leave. There was no way that Mom could afford to buy a house, so she started to look for a live-in job. By the time my school broke up for the summer holidays, she had found one.

On a wet Saturday afternoon I walked down the lane from Swayle Farm to the livery yard where I kept my pony, Tess, to break the news to my friends that I was moving away. I had known Virginia Barker and Richard Mason all my life. We were in the same form at Winterford Comprehensive School, we belonged to the same branch of the Pony Club, we competed together at gymkhanas and horse shows, and we spent as much time as possible at the Rectory Stables with all our other horse-obsessed friends. I would miss Ginny and Rich dreadfully but, even more, I would miss Tess.

Tess would not be able to come with us. Mom knew how much the pony meant to me and would never dream of making me sell her, but dear Tess, with her gentle ways and comical black and white markings, was getting on in years now. Although I steadfastly refused to admit it, I was growing far too tall for her. Mom could barely afford to keep one pony, yet alone buy and keep a bigger horse for me as well, so I just kept on hitching my stirrup leathers up another hole and pretending my legs were shorter than they were. Nevertheless, one day I would have to face the problem of what to do with Tess and, if I had to leave her behind at the Rectory, that day would not be long in coming.

Tess was waiting for me at the paddock gate, covered in mud where she had rolled and with rain dripping from her chin. Today might be our last ride together for a long time, and I cuddled her neck and felt miserable as I led her to her stable. I could hear Rich whistling in the box next door as he strapped his new horse, Mr. Big, a 16-hand chestnut. Like me, Rich had grown suddenly taller, and he had been forced to exchange his much loved pony, The Wizard, for a bigger mount. Rich was lucky, though, because he had found a good loan home for The Wizard, so he didn't have to sell him. Perhaps, given luck and time, I could do the same for Tess.

"Is that you, Anna?" Rich called, above the noise of rain drumming on the roof. Before I could reply, there was a clatter in the yard and Ginny sprinted across the cobbles leading her 14.2 hands high, milk-white pony, Pearly. Pearly was a bouncy, exuberant little mare, inclined at times to slightly lunatic behavior and capable of finding mud even on a dry day. This day she was plastered in it.

"Look at her!" Ginny grumbled, as the two of them dived for the shelter of Pearly's box. "Fine for you, Anna. At least Tess doesn't have an obsession with rolling in mud because of some primal instinct to camouflage herself. Anna? You are in there, aren't you?"

I heard Pearly's stable door slam, and then Ginny thrust her head over Tess' door and peered at me through her mass of drenched, flaming red hair. Ginny was petite and small-boned, so short that she had to stand on tip-toe to see over the half door. Ginny looked very fragile and helpless but, as anyone who knew her soon found out, appearances can be deceptive. She was about as fragile and helpless as a Sherman tank. She didn't suffer fools gladly and had a temper as hot as the color of her hair, but she was a great friend to have, especially in a crisis.

"Anna, what's wrong?" Ginny demanded. "You've got a face like a wet weekend!"

"It is a wet weekend," I said flippantly, not quite managing to hide my hurt.

"Your Mom has found a job at last and you are moving away?" Rich guessed. He appeared at the door behind Ginny, towering above her. He had kind eyes under a shock of brown hair, and people often thought, mistakenly, that he was dull and serious, but he seemed quiet only in comparison with Ginny. He had, in fact, a sharp sense of humor and remarkable strength of character that made him more than able to handle Ginny's mercurial temper. Their occasional, spectacular arguments were legendary.

7

"The horses will have to dry off before we can saddle them, so why not have a coffee and talk about it?" Ginny suggested.

I was glad to find the tack room almost deserted. Cathy Trent, whose mother owned the yard, was cleaning tack, while her brother Charlie, a renowned horse hater seldom seen in the stables, was breaking-in a new cricket bat by bashing it with a mallet, and grumbling that the village cricket match had been rained off.

"It can rain till doomsday, for all I care," I muttered.

"As bad as that?" Rich asked. He filled the kettle and spooned instant coffee into five mugs. "Come on, tell all."

"Mom got a job at the Manor House in Pikersfield. Two jobs really, as housekeeper for a guy called Hyde-Grant and as a nurse for his invalid daughter, Melissa. It all happened in a rush, and he wants us to move there tomorrow because he is going away. We'll have to live in an apartment in the house, and I can't take Tess."

"Oh come on, Anna, it could be far worse!" Rich grinned his relief. "You might have ended up miles away. Pikersfield is less than an hour's ride, by the shortcut across Winterford Moor. You won't even have to change schools, so it's hardly moving away."

"But I'll have to leave Tess here," I wailed, "and it's miles by road. The bus is next to useless because it takes hours to go around all the villages between here and there, and the fare costs a packet. I'll hardly ever be able to come back to see you all, yet alone ride this summer."

"But why should Melissa Hyde-Grant need a nurse?" Cathy broke in.

"I don't know. I've never met her."

"Yes you have. You know, the blonde girl in the first form. She has something wrong with her leg, so she doesn't do games, and she has asthma. I had to take her to the nurse once, when she had an attack."

"I know who you mean," Ginny said. "And if you ask me, she's a bit odd – doesn't get along with anyone and she has an awful temper."

"Pot calling the kettle black!" Rich remarked.

"Anyway," Ginny carried on, ignoring him. "I can't see why a limp and asthma need a full-time nurse. Melissa always looks pretty healthy to me."

"An asthmatic attack can be very nasty," Rich pointed out, with his usual sympathetic concern for other people's troubles. "Perhaps she suddenly got worse, or has been taken seriously ill."

"All the better for Anna!" Ginny's heart was not as soft as Rich's. "Not that I don't feel sorry for her too," she hastened to add, "but if your mom is busy being a full-time nurse, Anna, that will leave you free to spend the holidays here."

"You're welcome to stay with us," Cathy offered.

"Not possible, but thanks all the same," I said, with painful regret. "I'm part of the reason why Mr. Hyde-Grant chose Mom for the job. He thinks Melissa needs someone more her own age to keep her company and amuse her, because she spends so much time in bed. That's me, I'm the companion."

"Oh poor you!" Ginny groaned.

I had to admit that having to spend hours a day in a sickroom was a far from pleasant prospect, especially in the summer, when the alternative was to be riding Tess with my friends. On the other hand, I knew I was being selfish. Mom had to earn our living and we both needed somewhere to live, so it was only fair that I should do my share to help her. Besides which, there was this picture forming in my mind, of the pretty little girl with her blonde ringlets spread across her pillow – I had by now remembered Melissa and put a face to the name – sick, frail, and pathetically grateful for my company. I explained this to the others.

"How frightfully virtuous of you," Ginny chuckled. "But I have the nasty feeling that your emotions are running away with you! From what I've seen of Melissa Hyde-Grant, I don't think Saint Anna Hurst, visitor of the sick, will want to wear her halo for very long!"

Chapter Two

Everything had happened so quickly that the first I saw of Pikersfield Manor was the next day when we moved in. Mom had been to the house before, for the interview at which Mr. Hyde-Grant had offered her the job, so she had told me what to expect. It was a very old house, she said, full of very old furniture and, to her chagrin, rather gloomy and depressing. But I liked old places and old things. I found it fascinating to cross an ancient threshold and wonder who had crossed it before me long ago, or to touch an antique object and wonder what kind of person had handled it before me in the distant past. Nevertheless, I was quite unprepared for the strange effect that the Manor House was to have on me the minute I saw it.

Pikersfield was not a very attractive village. In fact, it had grown too big to be called a village, and was more like a sprawling little town. We threaded our way through a new estate, driving past row upon row of identical red brick boxes that lined the maze of identical-looking streets. The original hamlet of thatched cottages, a little Saxon church and an ancient inn called the Clarendon Arms had been swallowed by the developers' handiwork that swept, like an engulfing tide, right up to the gates of Pikersfield

Manor. The contrast of passing through those gates was like stepping back several hundred years in time.

The old house was hidden from its mass of new neighbors by tall iron gates set in a high brick wall, and then a stretch of neglected looking gardens. The drive curved between a tangle of overgrown shrubs and gnarled old trees that gave way to shaggy lawns. In front of the house was a knot garden, where rioting herbs—their stems woody with age—threatened to burst through the maze of low, clipped box hedges. A haze of blue-gray lavender bushes had all but taken over the paved terrace above the knot garden, and behind all rose the golden stone pile of Pikersfield Manor House.

It was a large house, rambling into several extensions that had been built onto it over the centuries of its life, but it did not strike me as grand or intimidating. It would have been homely and welcoming had it not seemed so sad. At its heart was the oldest part of the house, built of honey-gold stone with mullioned, latticed windows and tall, twisty chimneys. I was drawn to the place but, at the same time, strangely disturbed by it. Immediately, I felt the overwhelming conviction that the outward beauty and tranquility of the Manor was hiding some tragic secret, and I was uneasy with the sudden sensation that someone or something here, perhaps even the house itself, was expecting me. But the feeling passed and was forgotten when Mom turned the car into a courtyard behind the house.

Some distance from the front gates, the drive branched into two. The right-hand fork became a sweep of gravel that led to the front of the house. The left-hand fork curved behind the house, under a gate arch and into a courtyard surrounded by buildings. The buildings on the gate arch side of the yard were obviously garages, but the rest, on the other three sides of the cobbled square, looked to me suspiciously like stables. They were not the modern kind of stables, with half doors onto the yard, but the old-fashioned type with loose boxes behind the big double doors of the internal walkways.

"Wow, just look at this – stables! There must be dozens of them, and none of them used!" I scrambled out of the car, hardly daring to believe my eyes. I had glimpsed an orchard with fields beyond, at the end of the drive, so there must be grazing here too. I felt a surge of resentment at having to leave Tess behind when there was plenty of room for her at Pikersfield Manor.

"Sorry Anna, I told you we couldn't bring her." Mom guessed what I was thinking. "Mr. Hyde-Grant was very firm about it. Melissa is allergic to horse hair." Mom had reversed her car into a garage, and she led the way to where the back wing of the house met the yard, close to the gate arch. Ivy festooned down the gable end of one wing of the stables that appeared to be built onto the house, and a well, with a blocked-up top under its rotting winding gear, stood to one side of a massive, studded oak back door.

Now was not the time to argue, but maybe Mr. Hyde-Grant was the kind of man who could be persuaded or charmed into changing his mind – if I played my cards right! After all, Melissa never needed to come into contact with Tess. Even if Ginny was saving us the full livery charge by looking after Tess for me, it was ridiculous that Mom should have to go on paying the fees when there was free board and lodging here. Added to which, it made me miserable to think of Tess calling over her door to Ginny in the morning, and forgetting all about me.

The door was answered by a plump, bustling, elderly woman who introduced herself as "Mrs. Poppy", then led the way along the stone flagged passageways of the kitchen quarters to the front hall, where she left us to wait while she told Mr. Hyde-Grant of our arrival. The wide hallway was darkly paneled and, on all sides, the painted eyes of long dead people wearing antique costumes gazed down from their heavy, gilded frames. The only furniture was a carved oak coffer, that glowed with the patina of age-long polishing, and a longcase clock, that ticked slowly and majestically into the dim silence. Once again, I was struck by the weird feeling that I was expected.

At the end of the hall, a staircase rose under the jewel light of a stained glass window that depicted a family crest and, as I glanced around trying to make sense of my un-ease, my eye caught a portrait that hung at the foot of the stairs. The picture was of a young, very beautiful girl. Her startlingly blue eyes had been painted with such skill that they seemed to look straight at me and follow me. I couldn't help but be drawn irresistibly closer.

The girl's merry, laughing expression was strangely at odds with the conviction of sadness that I felt as I looked at her. The happy face was framed by a carefully arranged fringe of curls and an extravagant feather, that trimmed her wide-brimmed hat and swept down to mingle with the golden ringlets that tumbled about her shoulders. Her gown was of deep blue velvet that matched her eyes, and a string of milky pearls glowed at her throat. Her wide collar, and the cuffs that rose stiffly from her slender wrists, were of the finest lace. A plaque hanging below the portrait read "Melissa Anne Grant. 1636." I had a feeling that I had seen the face before, but surely that was not possible.

"I see you are admiring my mystery ancestress. She is lovely, isn't she?"

The man had come silently to the foot of the stairs and

his voice made me jump. With a sinking heart, I realized that he must be Mr. Hyde-Grant and that I had never met anyone who looked less charming or persuadable. He was tall, thin and stooped, as if he spent his whole life bending over to peer at things. Later I was to find out that he spent his time doing just that: pouring over dry-as-dust documents in old libraries all on his own. His eyes were cold, his expression grim, and there was no warmth in his voice, even as he claimed the beautiful, laughing girl as his ancestor.

"That picture is something of a puzzle," he said. "It was painted by Van Dyke at the court of King Charles 1. The girl lived in a magnificent Jacobean mansion that stood once on the site of the new Pikersfield estate, but the mansion was burnt down by Oliver Cromwell's soldiers and Melissa Anne vanished. She never lived in this house of course. This house was a far more humble dwelling than her own home, just a small manor house that the Grant family rented to a cousin, so no one knows why her portrait ended up here, but it did. The Grants were supporters of the king, Royalist Cavaliers – you know all about the English Civil War, of course."

It was not a question, it was a statement. I racked my brains, trying to recall history lessons about the Stuart King who had his head chopped off, but I couldn't remember much, not even why, or if, he had deserved it. Fortunately for me, I didn't have to display my ignorance because Mr. Hyde-Grant did not pursue the matter.

"My daughter was named after the Melissa in the portrait, there is a striking resemblance," he told me, turning away. "Come, we will take tea in the parlor. There are certain things, Mrs. Hurst, that both you and your daughter MUST understand."

I felt a little foolish for inventing a mystery where there

was none. I had seen the portrait face before only because it belonged also, as I now remembered, to the girl whom I'd taken little notice of—blonde-haired, attractive, Melissa Hyde-Grant. Some people have all the luck, I thought, with a touch of envy triggered by the fact that my mousy-brown hair refuses to curl. I am plain, but I am fit and healthy and Melissa, for all her fine home and good looks, was neither, which was proof that I should count my blessings and be content – or, at least, try to be.

Mr. Hyde-Grant led the way into a room where the afternoon sun, clear and fresh after the rain of yesterday, streamed through the lattices of a bay window. The air was heady with the scent of rambling roses, that rioted outside the mullions and dappled the golden light across a massive stone fireplace and wide, polished floorboards. Mom and I sat on the edges of antique chairs embroidered with faded petit-point, while Mrs. Poppy served us tea and very thin cucumber sandwiches.

"My daughter Melissa does not enjoy good health." Mr. Hyde-Grant addressed us as if he were giving a lecture. "She suffers frequent, very bad asthmatic attacks, and she was born with a disabling deformity of her right leg. This means that she is confined to her room for most of the time and needs constant attention. Above all she must never – do you understand, *never* – be stressed. The slightest upset brings on one of her attacks that must be treated at once. She MUST have her inhaler with her at all times; there is an oxygen cylinder beside her bed and sometimes she needs a nebulizer. Naturally, you know how to deal with all that, Mrs. Hurst?"

My mother had trained as a nurse before she married, so she was nodding her understanding. I was puzzled that Mr. Hyde-Grant made no mention of a sudden, serious illness

16

that made it all-at-once-necessary for Melissa to have a live-in nurse. Her limp and asthma had never seemed to trouble Melissa much at school. It occurred to me that there was something odd about the Hyde-Grant household but, I could not figure out what.

"And the little girl's mother?" Mom said hesitantly, as if she had been screwing up the courage to ask. "I understand that she never visits Melissa, and surely that can't be right? A sick child needs a mother, you know."

"That is exactly why you are here," Mr. Hyde-Grant snapped impatiently. "My wife and I are divorced, and she prefers to live abroad. My research work at Oxford University keeps me away from home most of the time. Melissa will be entirely your responsibility."

It did not sound as if Mr. Hyde-Grant cared very much about his invalid only child after all, despite his instructions that she should be so carefully looked after. His tone was just as cold and unemotional as it had been when he was talking about the girl in the portrait. I had the impression that his mind was on something else, and that my mother, myself, even his daughter, were merely irritating inconveniences. I was beginning to dislike Mr. Hyde-Grant and to feel very sorry for Melissa. After all, I knew exactly how it felt to lose a parent and Melissa had, in effect, lost both of hers.

Mom looked upset, not because she had been snapped at, but because she was a very caring person with a great capacity for love. She should have dozens of children instead of just me, and I could see that she was getting ready to lavish all her pent-up maternal instincts, pity, and affection on Melissa Hyde-Grant. I wondered how I would cope with having to share my mother with someone else, and I tried to suppress a pang of unreasonable jealousy.

"And you, Anna Hurst!" I stiffened to attention. Mr. Hyde-Grant had that effect on people. "You will spend part of every day with Melissa, to keep her company and amuse her. Mrs. Poppy will take you to her room to meet her now. And remember, Melissa must not be upset – complete calm at all times."

I followed Mrs. Poppy down even more flagstone-floored passages, through creaking oak doors, and up a rear stair-case. Our steps echoed on the bare oaken treads. Brass candlesticks and pewter plates gleamed dully on carved, polished surfaces. Dark canvasses in heavy frames hung on the walls below low, beamed ceilings. It looked as if nothing had changed at Pikersfield Manor for a very long time.

The landing was dimly lit and, as I followed my guide, a very strange thing happened. Suddenly I seemed to hear the swish of long skirts across the floor, and the clink of keys hanging from a housewife's belt. A trick of the light changed the figure in front of me to that of a modestly gowned woman holding aloft a candle. The white shapes of a starched cuff, a wide, plain collar and a Puritan cap glimmered in its light. Everything swayed as the candle flame swayed, rippling shadows across the linenfold paneling of the landing wall, and bending the shadow arm hugely across the ceiling. From the other side of the paneling, I thought I caught the muffled sound of sobbing. The scent of lavender, as faint and elusive as the sound of crying, drifted in the air.

I stopped dead in my tracks. The right-hand wall of the landing was blank, without doors or windows and, as far as I could judge after all the twists and turns we had taken, was no more than the back wall of the house. And yet I felt compelled to turn towards it, to reach out to touch it, seeking the source of the voice and the perfume. As my fingers met cold wood, the sound, the scent and the candle lights were gone.

Confused, I spun round. In the blink of an eye, Mrs. Poppy was just Mrs. Poppy again, wearing a flowered pinafore and with her bunions bulging out of her slippers. She appeared to have noticed nothing unusual and she gestured impatiently for me to catch up, as she turned a corner, crossed another landing and flung open a door. Her face stiffened, then with dislike, Mrs. Poppy shouted, "Here's the young lady that's come to keep you company, Melissa."

After the shock of what I had just experienced – or imagined I experienced – on the back landing, it took me a minute or two to absorb the further shock of Melissa's bedroom. Compared with the antique beauty of the rest of the house, it came as a horrible blow to the senses. The room echoed the pleasing proportions of the parlor below it, with the same mullioned bay window, a cushioned window seat, a great stone fireplace and a plaster-molded ceiling, but all had been what I could only describe as vandalized. The Tudor roses and mythical beasts of the ceiling were painted with garish, clashing colors, and the noble stone fireplace was covered in aerosol paint, viciously swirled and blotched all colors of the rainbow. Pop music crashed from the speakers of a monster hi-fi system.

Melissa Hyde-Grant scowled at us from her crumpled bed. She flicked a remote control, to reduce the decibels to a level that made conversation just about possible, and gave a vicious shove to a tray on the bedside table. A plate of sandwiches somersaulted onto the floor and scattered themselves, butter-side down, across the carpet.

"Take that muck back to the kitchen, Popeye, you know I hate cucumber!" she yelled at the elderly woman.

I expected Mrs. Poppy to protest at such rudeness, but she said nothing. Impassively, but with her mouth set in a hard line, she gathered up the debris, stacked it on the tray, and left the room.

"And you can get out too. I don't want you here!" Melissa glared at me. She was not a pretty sight. Her neglected, greasy hair hung in rats' tails about her shoulders, and her dirty nightdress was spotted with food stains.

I was at a loss for words. There was nothing weak or pathetic about the way the invalid flounced off her bed and flung herself down on the window seat with her back to me. I could feel her hostility vibrating right across the room. Nevertheless, I owed it to my mother to make an effort to get along with her, so I hunted up the remote control, turned off the TV, and sat down beside her.

"Mind your own business and leave my things alone. I said I don't want you here, so push off," Melissa said, nastily.

"Well, I'm sorry, but your dad has given my mom the job of looking after you, so there is nothing either of us can do about it. You might as well make the best of it."

"Hasn't he told you I get ill when I'm upset?" she demanded. "Now that my father is home I don't need anyone to look after me, so if you don't go away I will get upset, and then I will be ill, and you will get the blame."

Melissa scrambled back onto her bed and punched the hi-fi remote until the speakers shuddered with noise. The pity I felt for her was suddenly replaced by utter dislike. As Ginny had predicted, I was not going to wear my halo for long. I leaned across the bed, shouting at her so she could hear me above the TV.

"It sounds to me as if you WANT to be ill. Do you enjoy getting upset or what?"

20

I was speaking in anger without really thinking, but I could see that I had touched a raw nerve by the way Melissa was staring at me, surprise and horror, guilt and fury written all over her face. It made me suspicious. Was there some reason why Melissa really did want to be ill? Had she been pretending all along? If so, I thought with satisfaction, she would not be able to fool my mother for long.

"I – hate – you," Melissa growled, with a gasping breath between each word. "You are as beastly as Popeye and all the others. No one ever feels sorry for ME."

"I'm not surprised, if this is the way you behave!" Again I spoke in anger. I should have had more self-control.

Melissa was panting rapidly now. Seconds later she began to wheeze and choke. She slumped back onto the bed, looking at the point of suffocating collapse, but her hand was reaching strongly for the bedside bell. Her summons was answered by the sound of running feet.

A grim-faced Mr. Hyde-Grant rushed into the room, closely followed by Mrs. Poppy and my mother. Mom tried to force the inhaler between Melissa's clenched teeth, but the girl thrashed about so wildly that Mom gave up and pushed the oxygen mask over her face. Mr. Hyde-Grant spun me around by the shoulders and roughly propelled me, out of the room.

"I warned you!" he said.

I did not need his lecture to make me feel guilty. It was true that I had upset Melissa, and he had indeed warned me that when Melissa was upset the stress brought on an asthmatic attack. Or did it? I was sure that Melissa was pretending to be ill.

Chapter Three

"Tan Madam Melissa's backside, that's what I'd do, given half a chance!" Mrs. Poppy slapped rashers of bacon into the pan as if warming up her arm in readiness. She had arrived while I was wandering around the kitchen looking for something to eat, and she insisted on cooking me a big breakfast to cheer me up. She had been witness to most of what had happened the night before, and it turned out that in Mrs. Poppy I had found an unexpected but very welcome ally.

Melissa had become so ill that, in the end, even I had to admit she was not pretending. She was fighting for her breath and her lips were turning blue. Mom was so worried that she phoned the doctor. Both she and Mr. Hyde-Grant held me entirely to blame, and I was sent to my room in disgrace.

The housekeeper's apartment was upstairs in the Georgian extension at the far end of the house. It appeared that Mr. Hyde-Grant's obsession with the past did not, fortunately, extend to plumbing and modern conveniences. The apartment was very comfortable, with two bedrooms, a sitting room, and bright, well-equipped kitchen and bathroom. As in the rest of the house, the furniture was all antique, beautiful and valuable, and my bedroom boasted a four poster bed that I fell in love with at once. My window looked out across rose-bordered lawns and, if I craned my neck to the left, I could just see the stable yard where it joined the kitchen wing at the back of the house.

Given other circumstances I would have thought myself lucky to live in such a place, but now, having met Melissa, I could see nothing but problems and unpleasantness ahead. Mom immediately moved all her things into the room next to Melissa's, so that she could answer Melissa's bell more quickly and be close enough to constantly keep an eye on her. I stayed in the apartment by myself that night and felt lonely.

"Always the same, she is, want this, demand that and never a civil word for anyone!" Mrs. Poppy was still in full flow. "Very convenient, them attacks. That's what I say. Dozens of housekeepers we've had here, dozens! But they don't stay long because they won't put up with Madam's tantrums, and who can blame them? I'd go too, except my Ted won't hear of it. My Ted does the garden, when he has a mind to, but after all those years digging and bending, his back pains him."

"Has he worked here a long time then, Mrs. Poppy?" I asked, as she paused for breath and put a plate in front of me. "Oh, thank you very much. The eggs are just how I like them." She beamed her pleasure, as if not used to being thanked.

"There's been Poppy's working at the Manor House time out of mind!" There was a touch of pride in her voice, despite her obvious scorn for the present occupants of the house. "My Ted's dad and his dad before him, not that my Ted has much time for Mr. H-G's fanciful notions. Mad about Cavaliers and some old civil war is Mr. H-G, cranky about history and stuff. Obsessed, he is, about keeping the house looking just like it did in them days. He never gives a thought to how much polishing all that old furniture and brass clutter makes for me. Less pride and a touch of honest hard work would do him good, instead of all his day-dreaming!"

Mrs. Poppy's puritan streak was showing, and I wondered about the trick of the light, the night before, that had revealed her momentarily to me in severe Puritan garb. Perhaps the old house was playing tricks on us all. Obviously the house had already become an unhealthy obsession with Mr. Hyde-Grant, so maybe, also, it was driving Melissa out of her mind.

"What do you mean about Melissa's attacks being convenient?" I asked.

"Just what I says, very convenient when she can't get her own way, or when she thinks folks aren't paying her enough attention. She never used to have them that bad or that often. I'd say she was after having us on most of the time. She's a play-acting phony, that's what Melissa is, a phony!"

"That's a wicked thing to say, Mrs. Poppy." My mother came into the kitchen looking tired and harassed. "There was nothing phony about Melissa's attack last night. I should know. I've nursed asthmatics before."

Mrs. Poppy snorted her scorn and muttered something about speaking as she found. She gave me a conspiratorial wink and a kindly pat on the shoulder. Mom was laying a tray and warming milk as she said, "What the poor child needs is love and understanding. More than anything, she needs a mother – and her father is not much good! He was off back to Oxford first thing this morning, even though his daughter is so ill."

"All Mr. H-G wants is peace and quiet to stick his head

back in his books," Mrs. Poppy observed. "He wasn't upset because he felt sorry for Melissa's wheezing and gasping. He was just put out because someone had given her yet another excuse to get herself all steamed up and interrupt what he was doing."

"Yes, Anna." Mom frowned at me. "How could you have been so callous as to accuse Melissa of pretending to be ill?"

Melissa had not been too breathless to tell her father, with a few invented embellishments, exactly how I had upset her.

"Don't you go blaming Anna now, Mrs. Hurst," Mrs. Poppy protested. "You don't want to believe half of what Melissa says, and I should know."

Mom looked troubled and ran her hand distractedly through her hair saying, "Oh dear, I don't know what to believe."

I felt guilty because what Melissa had said was exactly what I had been thinking. I was too confused and uncertain to understand my own feelings, yet alone explain them to Mom, so I just kept quiet.

"Melissa needs help," Mom said. "I'm sure her 'getting all steamed up' as you call it, Mrs. Poppy, is just that, a cry for help, and something should be done about it."

"That's as may be," Mrs. Poppy sniffed, "but there's never been anything her mom and dad have ever done that's helped. It broke Mr. H-G's heart it did, having to sell off the land to the developers for that new estate, just so he could afford to keep the old Manor House going. 'Melissa's inheritance,' he calls it, and he buys her every last thing she wants. Anything she wants she has, and he won't let no one cross her, and it's spoiled her rotten. And the pity is, she don't even love him for it. She wrecked her room just to spite him. Now he keeps out of her way as much as possible, and there's few who would blame him."

"Well I do," Mom snapped. "He can't expect to bribe her into loving him. Money buys only things, not happiness. Melissa needs someone to care about her, not a grand, empty house full of expensive nothing. I'll sit with her all day today. You've caused enough trouble already, Anna, so you'd better keep out of the way. I'm sure you can find something to do with yourself."

I left the house feeling miserable. It hurt that my mother should think so badly of me, especially as there had never before been a hard word between us. Knowing that I had brought it on myself only made matters worse.

But where to go? I didn't have enough money for the bus fare to Swallowbridge, and the idea of wandering around the Pikersfield estate all day didn't exactly thrill me. I drifted across the paved terrace in front of the house, where lavender bushes grew in such profusion, all around the edges and sprawling across the stones. They were not yet in full flower but, when I picked a handful of buds and crushed them between my fingers, they gave off a sweet scent.

"Lavender is for peace and tranquility, so I guess you'll be having a need for it Miss." The voice came from beyond the terrace balustrade, and I looked down to see an old man leaning on his fork in the overgrown knot garden. He wore a moleskin waistcoat and cord trousers tucked into Wellington boots. I guessed he was My Ted.

"Good morning Mr. Poppy. Is your back feeling better today?"

He looked startled but pleased. "'Tis only middling, but kind of you to ask. A little politeness is a rare and welcome thing hereabouts. Though I doubt you'll be so chipper for long, mind. This place will get to you too in the end," he prophesied enigmatically.

"What do you mean, 'get to me?'"

"'Tis the lovage plant what helps my back. Good for all manner of strains is lovage." He evaded my question.

"Do you mean Pikersfield Manor will get to me?"

"An herb to cure every ill, there is. I tell my Missis, infusion of marjoram, that would help young Melissa's nerves. Feverfew for her headaches, hyssop and garlic for her chest, but nobody ever listens to me."

"I'm not surprised if you never answer a question, or do you always talk in riddles?"

"Oh, you're a direct one alright," the old man chuckled. "But you put that lavender under your pillow, 'twill help you sleep peacefully at night."

"I always sleep well, unless you know a reason why I shouldn't!" I was getting angry, but Mr. Poppy merely laughed at my sharpness.

"It don't do nobody no good, living in the past, not in this house of tears any road."

"I have no intention of living in the past," I retorted.

"Happen you'll get no choice. There's that about Pikersfield Manor House as has the power of getting its own way."

I didn't know why I suddenly felt the need to share my premonition with a stranger, but I found myself blurting out, "The minute I arrived, I had the strangest feeling that the house was expecting me."

"Aye, could be that it is," Mr. Poppy said, thoughtfully. "Maybe time has come full circle at last, to set all in place and bring the tears to an end."

I could only assume that he must be referring to the unhappy child, Melissa. Mr. Hyde-Grant had intended my company to cheer her up but, now, that seemed highly unlikely.

"I don't think Melissa likes me very much, if that's what you mean," I laughed.

"Happen I do, happen I don't, and I'm not saying which one either. Any road, I've got work to do, so you run along and leave me be." Mr. Poppy turned back to his digging and ignored me until I went away.

I had met people like Mr. Poppy before, people who liked to make the mundane things they had to say sound more important by dressing them up in mystery and double meaning. Stripped of the herb lore and enigma, all Mr. Poppy really had to say was that living in a house with Melissa Hyde-Grant would depress me, and he was not far wrong!

Which brought me back to my present problem – to get as far away from Melissa as possible. I decided to explore what lay behind the Manor House, so I made my way back down the drive. I glanced into the stable yard as I passed.

It was obvious that horses hadn't lived there for many years. It was obvious, too, that the four long wings, enclosing the cobbled court, had not been built all at the same time. The wing on the right hand side of the yard, the nearest end of which butted up hard against the back wing of the house, looked as ancient as the house itself and almost derelict. The other two stable blocks were in better repair, the left hand one being a lofty, handsome building. The garages along the gate arch side of the yard were fairly modern.

Unfortunately, I could see very little through the grimy, cobwebbed windows. All the outer doors, that led into the internal walkways that served the loose boxes, were bolted and padlocked shut. I could see no way into anywhere except the garages, and I was not interested in them.

Nevertheless, I decided it would be worth poking around one day soon. I refused to give up the idea of finding a way to bring Tess to Pikersfield Manor. My plan of getting around Mr. Hyde-Grant was, obviously, a non-starter, but there are usually more ways than one of solving any problem.

At the end of the drive, where it turned under the arch, there was a five-bar gate into an orchard. The grass under the trees was long, and clumps of nettles and brambles, that had been only partially cleared, were re-sprouting their triumph over My Ted's back. Beyond the orchard stretched a wide vista of sheep-cropped fields. It was as if Pikersfield Manor, stuck in its time warp and sheltering its strange, sad people, was a dam that held at bay both the developers' flood tide and the modern world.

I crossed several fields full of sheep, climbed a gate and found myself in a lane. A sign pointed to Pikersfield, one mile to the left, and Winterford Moor, one mile to the right. I turned towards the moor and began to walk briskly under a hot sun.

It was a wretched, miserable creature, but it was a horse so I stopped to look at it. He was a tall horse, over 16.2 hands high I guessed, and he would have been strikingly handsome had he not been in such poor condition. His coat was an eye-catching color, deeply dappled iron gray and white, with points, mane and tail so richly black that they looked almost navy blue in the sunshine. But he was pitifully thin. His ribs stood out clearly beneath his staring hide and he was crawling with lice. He was struggling to push his nose under the broken bottom rail of the gate, to reach the grass on the roadside verge.

I pulled a clump of succulent green from the verge, and

the horse made a grab for it. No wonder he was starving. His small paddock was bare of grass and sour with weeds and droppings. He must have been left there, neglected, for a long time because his unkempt mane tangled down to below his shoulder, his bur-stuck tail swept the ground and his cracking hooves were badly overgrown. His water trough was practically dry.

I glanced up and down the lane. There was not a house or even a farm in sight, and no clue as to whom the horse belonged. I tore up an armful of grass, threw it over the gate, then climbed into the field while he was eating. I knew nothing about the horse's temperament, so it was best not to take chances.

The trough cistern was choked with dead leaves, that had jammed the ball-cock to shut off more than a seepage of water. It did not take me long to free it. The trickle became a gush and, at the sound of running water, a gray muzzle pushed under my arm and sucked thirstily.

"You poor, poor horse," I said. He flicked an ear and nudged his face gently against my chest. I rubbed his nose. He had large, dark, generous eyes and a little pink snip between his nostrils. My heart ached for him. Cruel, ignorant people had made his life a misery, but he didn't hold a grudge against humankind and was prepared to like and trust me. He must be a very good- natured horse indeed.

Then the horse flung up his head and whinnied at the sound of hoof beats along the lane. If the rider was the gray horse's owner, they were about to feel the sharp edge of my tongue. I couldn't believe my eyes when Pearly and Mr. Big jogged into sight.

"Ginny, Rich!" I stood on the gate, waving my excitement to catch their attention. I hadn't dared hope to see them again so soon.

"We were riding across the moor," Ginny called, "so decided to do the extra couple of miles to see how you are doing. Good grief, what on earth is that?" She stood in her stirrups and peered over the hedge. The gray horse raised his dripping muzzle from the trough, then ambled towards the gate. "Yuck, it's covered in LICE!" Ginny backed Pearly quickly away.

"Not a bad-looking horse, all the same," Rich observed. "In fact, it could be a stunner – nicely put together, good bone."

"I can see all his bones!" Ginny exclaimed. "Someone is going to have to do something about him. It looks like he's got a belly full of worms which means he'll be a gonner soon."

We tethered Pearly and Mr. Big on the opposite verge, well away from the gray horse's lice, and pulled more grass for him to eat.

"I was thinking about just that before you turned up," I said, "and I've a good mind to rescue him myself." The gray horse paused in his chewing to lip at my hands, as if begging me to get on with it and do so. My mind was made up. The terrible state of the horse pulled at my heart, and I would have hauled him out of that beastly paddock and taken him back to Pikersfield Manor there and then, had Rich not stopped me.

"You can't do that, it's stealing! You'd be arrested for horsenapping."

"But, as Ginny said, something has to be done. I can't just walk away and leave him to suffer."

"Then get hold of the ASPCA," Rich told me, with annoying practicality.

Reluctantly, I had to admit that he was right. The best I could do, for the moment, was to ring the ASPCA as soon

31

as I got home, to report the condition and whereabouts of the neglected animal. At least he had, now, a little food and plenty of water.

We sat beside the tethered horses, in the shade of the hedge, and shared the sandwiches that Ginny and Rich had brought in their saddlebags. I told them of Melissa's asthma attack the night before, and why I was in trouble because of it.

"It sounds like nothing more than attention-seeking to me," Ginny said, as she carefully removed the crusts from her sandwiches and fed them to Pearly. "She knows that she can have everyone running round in small circles after her, and can get her own way by being ill, so off she goes, wheeze, wheeze, do as I say or else! I'd ignore her, if I were you. Show her it doesn't work."

"You can't ignore someone who is choking to death!" I protested.

"In this case, I could. Anyway, I thought you said she was only pretending."

"I'm not sure," I wailed. "At first I was sure, then seeing Melissa in such a state got me all confused. Now I don't know what to believe."

"Calm down and give yourself time," Rich advised. "After all, you've been there only 24 hours, and you'll need a lot longer than that to find out what makes Melissa tick. Just go along with anything she wants and keep the peace. Surely it's worth the hassle because, if your mom's job doesn't work out, you might have to move miles away and we'd never see you again. And you should eat your crusts, Sal. They are good for your teeth."

"That is as stupid as saying that eating carrots helps you to see in the dark!" Ginny defiantly passed her last crust to Pearly. Mr. Big, realizing that he was missing out on something, sidled to the end of his halter rope to investigate. Pearly swung round and sank her crust-improved teeth into his neck.

"Idiot!" Rick exclaimed. Ginny, assuming that Rich was referring to his horse and not to herself, left him to settle the ensuing scuffle by dividing his only apple between the two animals.

"Anyway," Ginny said, "if it makes Melissa happy to lie around all day, pretending to be at death's door, it's no skin off your nose, is it Anna?"

"Except that I'm expected to keep her company!" I pointed out, drearily. "I'll give it a whirl, but you two will have to turn up pretty often, just to keep me sane."

"Next time we'll bring Tess with us, that should cheer you up," Rich promised. He very deliberately took Ginny's apple from her lunch box and bit into it, scoring a victory on points.

In fact, they decided to come again the very next day and use Tess as a pack-horse. They would bring hay for the gray horse, plus louse powder and a dose of wormer, and we would be able to make a start on cleaning up his filthy paddock. With luck, I could persuade an ASPCA inspector to meet us at the field in the morning.

I watched my friends ride away and wished I was going with them. As they trotted around a bend in the lane and out of sight, the big chestnut cob was keeping a respectful distance between himself and the biting end of the diminutive white mare. It had not taken Mr. Big long to learn that no one trifled with Pearly, even if they were twice her size. Rich had long since discovered that the same applied to Ginny, but the cob, obviously, boasted a far less determined character than his new owner.

33

Chapter Four

I don't know what Mom said to Melissa, that day, but it seemed to have worked a minor miracle. Melissa's room was still a disturbing place to be – all those violent colors made me edgy, and the sight of the vandalized fireplace never failed to upset me. At least now it was tidy and the scent of roses coming from the open window had banished the stuffy smell of sickness.

Mom had washed and curled Melissa's long, blonde hair so that she looked very pretty and startlingly like the picture in the hall. It was uncanny, just as if Melissa Anne Grant had stepped out of her portrait. Melissa sat up in a freshly made bed, propped against a heap of pillows, and she was wearing MY best, lacy nightdress.

After her sleepless night and busy day, Mom looked exhausted, but she seemed happier than she had that morning. I offered to sit with Melissa while Mom had a relaxing hot bath and a rest. She hesitated, at first, and I was upset by her lack of trust.

"Whatever you do, keep her calm," she ordered. "Treat her very gently. She felt too poorly after her attack to eat anything today, and she is very weak. Her lack of appetite is an awful worry for me. Perhaps you can tempt her with something."

I solemnly promised to be the model of tact and, eventually, I managed to shoo Mom away to our apartment, out of earshot of Melissa's bell.

"Your hair looks very nice," I said, as I went into Melissa's room with biscuits and orange squash on a tray. She glanced up at me briefly, then looked down at her hands and picked idly at the satin trim of the duvet. "We got off on the wrong foot last night, Melissa, so let's start again, shall we? What would you like to do this evening?"

I glanced around the room, seeking inspiration. There were masses of CDs stacked beside the hi-fi, and I longed to look through them to see if there were any of my favorites. Glossy magazines, the sort I used to sneak through in the newsstand but could not afford, were piled on the window seat. The dressing table was littered with more expensive make-up than a 12-year-old girl could ever need, and with bottles of exotic perfume, the kind that you try but never buy in department stores. At the foot of the bed was the biggest television set I had ever laid eyes on, with a video recorder and a satellite decoder stacked underneath.

It was all very well for Mom to say that money can't buy happiness, but it could buy a whole heap of things that I could not have. I felt like a kid looking longingly through a toy store window. Rich was right. I must try to get along with Melissa – at least until I had had time to play her CDs, watch her videos, and use up some of her perfume. Then I felt guilty for thinking such mean thoughts.

"What would you like to do this evening?" I repeated.

"I like your mother. She did my hair and gave me a pretty nightgown." Melissa kept her head bent, scowling up at me under her eyelashes.

"Yes, Mom is great." I didn't mention the fact that it had

been MY nightgown, a pale blue silk and lace luxury of a birthday present from my aunt. I hadn't even worn it yet. Why should Melissa have it when she had wardrobes full of designer-label clothes?

"I like your mother," Melissa said again, pouting like a spoiled, small child half her age, "but I don't like you, so shut up and leave me alone."

I had no intention of giving Melissa the slightest excuse to get "all worked up'" again. I walked over to the window seat, picked up a fashion magazine, then settled down to read it. There was a long silence.

"What do you think you are doing?" Melissa demanded, eventually.

"Shutting up and leaving you alone, just as you told me to do."

"But you are *supposed* to be amusing me."

"You can't have it both ways."

Melissa looked confused, then cross. "You shouldn't up-set me, it makes me ill," she threatened. She took a deep breath.

"Just you try it, and I'll ring your bell myself. I'm sure Mom would like to see you start one of your attacks."

Melissa held her breath for a second, then suddenly let it out, hissing, "You pig. Now I REALLY hate you!"

"Fair enough, hate away. I'll tell you what I've been do-ing today."

"I couldn't care less. There's nothing to do in this dump anyway. Pikersfield is the pits, and this house is a moldy old museum."

I carried on regardless. "I found a horse that is starving to death because his owner has neglected him. I'm going to rescue him and give him a good home. When he is fit and well again, I'm going to ride him and take him to Pony

36

Club and shows. He is such a special horse that I'm sure he will win lots of rosettes."

This idea must have been brewing in my subconscious all day, and it was only when the words came out that I realized that it was exactly what I wanted to do. Fate had found me a bigger mount, and a very special one at that. Now there was only the problem to solve of what to do with elderly, outgrown Tess.

Quite by chance, I had stumbled upon something that interested Melissa. She made me tell her the story of the gray horse all over again, this time with every last detail. Then she wanted to know all about Tess, the Rectory Stables, Pony Club, horse shows, and Ginny and Rich. She scrambled out of bed and sat beside me, eating biscuits and slopping squash down the front of MY nightdress. The evening air was getting chilly, so I closed the window and fetched her a cardigan. Melissa actually said thank you.

"I wish I could learn to ride," she sighed, wistfully.

"It's not really possible, is it, if horse hair brings on your asthma?"

"It doesn't always." A sly expression flickered in her eyes.

Again I was suspicious. I had a friend in the Pony Club who was allergic to virtually everything with hair. Her eyes streamed and her chest wheezed before she came within feet of a horse, but she took her pills, used her inhaler, and endured the discomfort with a cheerful grin, because she wanted to ride. Perhaps the way to get Melissa over her hypochondria and get her out and about, was to make her want it badly enough. Besides which, the maxim "there is usually more than one solution to any problem" was proving to be true.

"I've almost outgrown Tess," I remarked, casually, "but

she would be just right for you to learn on. She is very quiet and gentle – perfect for a beginner. If I could have the use of a stable and the orchard, I could bring her here and teach you to ride."

Melissa's face lit up with joy. It was the first time I had seen her smile, and it was a vast improvement on the discontented glower. Melissa was far too excited to sit still. She jumped to her feet and skipped round the room, singing, "I'm going to learn to ride!" I noted that her limp seemed to hardly bother her .

"And that's another thing," I said. "Riding will do your leg good. It will build up muscles and make it stronger." Melissa gave me a sharp look and hobbled to the bed.

"I'll tell Daddy that. I'll write and ask him if you can bring Tess here." Then she added, as an afterthought, "but you can't use the stables. No one has used the stables for years because they are haunted." I burst out laughing.

"No, honestly Anna, they really are haunted. Surely you've heard of the Wailing Woman of Pikersfield?" I shook my head. "She's even in the County Guide Book! Daddy did a whole load of research and said the story was ridiculous, but my great, great grandfather heard her in the old stables. Not that he told me, of course, because he died years before I was born, but he told my great grandfather, and so on down. Even old man Popeye the gardener believes in her, because his great grandfather heard her too. The ghost was why the newer wings of the stable block were built, when the old one got too haunted to use."

By now the sun had gone down and the room was quite dark, to set the scene for a ghost story. I knew it was only make-believe, but I thought it would be amusing. Besides which, I had done all the talking so far, and it would do Melissa good to exercise her voice in something other than

38

grumbles and being rude to people. She was becoming more normal by the minute, and I was rather proud of myself. I lit the fancy candles on her dressing table and we sat cross-legged on the floor, giggling.

"It is a haunting by voice alone," Melissa began in sepulchral tones. I laughed again. "Don't keep laughing, Anna, you'll spoil it! It is, it's just a voice, a crying, sobbing, weeping, miserable voice."

"A man or a woman?"

"A girl, silly. Male ghosts don't sob, they moan. Anyway no one has ever seen anything, just heard the voice. There are written accounts of it going back hundreds of years. I think Daddy said the first was at about the time that King Charles II came home from exile, whenever that was. Lots of people heard the crying voice in the stables, and it had the power to make them dreadfully miserable. It would be quiet for years, then something would set it off again. It became known as the Wailing Woman of Pikersfield.

"For some reason, the ghost was particularly bothersome in my great, great grandfather's time. He was very keen on fox hunting and had dozens of horses, so it was not at all convenient when the ghost frightened all his grooms away. He took it seriously enough to have a priest come to do an exorcism, but it couldn't have worked because he stopped using the old stable block and built a new one."

"Which is the old stable block, then?" I asked.

"You know the arch with the clock over it?" I nodded. "Well, as you stand under the arch and look into the yard, immediately on your right you have the well and the scullery door, and then the building, built onto the back wing of the house at this end, that goes away up the yard on the right-hand side?" I nodded again. "That is the oldest wing of the stables, the haunted one."

"Which bit did your great, great grandfather build to replace it?"

"The block across the back of the yard, straight in front of you as you stand under the arch. The building down the left-hand side of the yard is newer still, designed by my great grandfather, who had even more horses and rather grand ideas. It's like a horsy palace inside. The garage block completed the square when cars were invented. "

I had, now, a pretty clear idea of how the higgledy-piggledy square of buildings round the courtyard had developed over the years, and why none of their roof levels or windows matched.

"So then what happened?"

"Nothing much. On dark and stormy nights, the voice could still be heard, wailing through the buildings!"

"You are making that bit up!"

"'Fraid so. It's a laugh, though."

"But who does, or did, the voice belong to?"

"Haven't a clue. I don't think anyone ever found out."

"Is the ghost still there?" I was disappointed that the story had come to such an abrupt end, and I was losing interest.

"Who knows?" Melissa grinned. "It hasn't been heard for years, but no one has used the stables for years. You might find out when you bring Tess here, but I doubt it. My father says that the Wailing Woman is no more than a silly folk legend, and he should know. He spends his life reading and writing about people who have been dead for centuries, which is stupid because it's people who are alive that matter, and he should care about them."

I was beginning to see the light. "Your father cares about you," I told her gently. "Why else would he give you everything you want?"

40

"He cares much more about this rotten old house!" There was a catch in Melissa's voice. "The only reason he ever comes here is to gloat over the place, or to bring it another bit of furniture that is 'in period', as he calls it. The only time he ever stayed here for very long was when he was writing its history and searching for the priest's hole. He was convinced that there had to be one because the Grants – they owned the house long ago, although they never lived in it – the Grants were Roman Catholics. When the Catholics were being persecuted, families like them made secret places for the priests to hide in. He never found one though. But, you see, he is only interested in people who lived long ago. I told him I hate history, and I hate this house."

"Is that why you messed up this lovely room?"

"Too true! He even wanted me to have an ugly old four poster bed that Charles I had slept in. I told him no way, and to hide it in the housekeeper's apartment. Then he kept on about how people must have stood in front of this fireplace and talked about Oliver Cromwell. I said let Oliver Cromwell rot, and I sprayed the monstrosity with aerosol paint."

Poor Melissa! This glimpse inside her tortured mind had given me the reason why she hated Pikersfield Manor so much: she was jealous of the place! It was tragic that Mr. Hyde-Grant could not show as much love for his daughter as he did for his historic home. But then, I thought to myself, Melissa was not particularly lovable.

Melissa's face had returned to its usual scowl and the disturbed look was back in her eyes. It was about time I changed the subject.

"Are you hungry?"

"Starving!"

41

"Right, let's have a midnight feast! We can watch a film while we eat. Do you have a movie channel?"

At the mention of a midnight feast, Melissa cheered up at once. She seemed very immature for her age. Perhaps it was the result of leading such a lonely life, looked after by a succession of disinterested housekeepers and Mrs. Poppy who, to be honest, heartily disliked her. I was only three years older than Melissa, but I could see that I was going to be more of a baby-sitter than a companion.

To my surprise, Melissa followed me down to the kitchen. We thoroughly enjoyed ourselves and made a great mess, concocting cheeseburgers topping them with every relish we could find, and making ice-cream sundaes from the well-stocked freezer. We carried our food back to Melissa's room, and watched the "Canterville Ghost" on "Movie Greats." It seemed a fitting way to end the evening.

"Are you going to see the gray horse tomorrow?" Melissa asked. She had cleared her plates with one of the healthiest appetites I had ever come across. I would have to reassure Mom that the invalid was unlikely to perish from famine just yet.

"Yes. A man from the ASPCA is meeting me at the field 10 a.m."

"You will come back right away and tell me what he says?"

"Yes, of course, and I'll be here with you all afternoon."

"Promise?"

"I promise."

"Cross your heart?"

"Oh go to bed, Melissa!"

I returned to the apartment with a light heart. I had managed to get through the whole evening without upsetting Melissa, who was now dead to the world, sleeping off her gargantuan feast. There was no need for me to wake Mom who, despite all the noise we had made, was fast asleep in the room next to Melissa's.

Things certainly looked a lot brighter now. Tess was more or less on her way to Pikersfield Manor, I had found my dream horse, Melissa had accepted me as a friend, and I was going to sleep in a four poster bed that King Charles I had once slept in. I wondered if he, too, had found the mattress a trifle lumpy. It would have been a lot more comfortable, though, than having his head chopped off!

Chapter Five

"Well, I really don't know!" Peter Sams, the ASPCA inspector, took off his cap and scratched his head in perplexity. "The poor beggar certainly needs food, no doubt about that but, technically, you kids are trespassing by going into his field and messing with him."

The gray was chomping his way through a pile of Ginny's best hay, and he was surrounded by a cloud of louse powder. Rich had rasped the worst of the cracking overgrowth from the horse's hooves, but the gray still urgently needed the attention of a qualified farrier.

"If the cruel, ignorant person who owns him wants to take me to court for trespassing, then they're more than welcome," I told Mr. Sams.

"And if you're not going to take him away and look after him, then we will keep on going into his paddock, and do whatever the horse needs!" Ginny agreed hotly.

"Alright, alright, give me a chance! I'll make inquiries about his owner, but I have to go through proper procedures. I'm not allowed to walk away with someone's horse whenever I feel like it. And if you keep up all this caring, feeding, and de-lousing, I won't have any evidence of neglect anyway!"

The inspector's grin told us he was joking, but I was already too emotionally involved with the horse to find it funny. Mr. Sams held the gray's head, while I pushed a plastic syringe between the horse's teeth and squirted a worming dose down his throat. The wormer would take care of the gut parasites he was bound to have, and would tackle the lice from the inside. The gray stuck his head in the air and wrinkled his lips, looking offended.

"If anyone asks me, I've never seen you trespassing, right? I'll let you know as soon as I find out who owns him. Keep up the good work." Mr. Sams climbed into his van and, with a cheerful wave, drove away.

I scrubbed my hands in a bucket of water and crossed the lane to make a fuss of Tess, who was tethered to the hedge on the far side of the wide verge, nose to nose with her friend Pearly. Mr. Big as resting a hind leg and pretending to be asleep, but I was sure he had half an eye warily on the little white mare. It was a couple of days since I'd last seen Tess and I didn't want her to think I was neglecting her for another horse, but she seemed even smaller after the tall gray. Now that the solution had presented itself to me, I could at last face the fact that I had outgrown Tess. If I could find a way to buy the gray, and to talk Mr. Hyde-Grant into having Tess on loan for Melissa, so that my dear old pony need never be sold, then all my problems would be over. I told Ginny and Rich of my plans.

"Too many ifs and buts," Ginny declared. "You can't count on anything Melissa says, and a sure-fire way to ruin the summer holidays is having to spend them teaching her to ride. She sounds like a spoiled baby to me."

Rich accused Ginny of being negative, defeatist, and unsympathetic. Ginny shouted back that she was entitled to her own opinion, and they seemed all set for one of their arguments. I yelled at them both to shut up.

"Look, I've got to deal with first things first," I said. "The ifs and buts won't matter anyway, if I can't buy the gray. I don't have a dime, so I'll have to find a holiday job. Any ideas?"

"Whatever you do, you'll never raise enough cash to buy him by the time Mr. Sams finds his owner," Rich reasoned. "And it wouldn't surprise me if the owner turns nasty and sends him to a horse sale right away. He might even have him put down to save time and trouble."

"Now who's being negative and defeatist?" Ginny snapped. "With the state he's in, the gray will fetch only peanuts at auction, and I'm sure Mr. Sams will stop them putting him down. If we ALL get a job, we'll earn enough money in no time. But WHAT job?"

"Fruit picking," Rich suggested. "Winterford Fruit Farm takes on casual labor at this time of year."

Ginny seized on his idea with enthusiasm. She declared that there was no time like the present, and was immediately tightening Pearly's girth and running down her irons. "If we ALL work to earn money to buy him," she said, "then we'll ALL be part owners of the gray. Won't that be fun?"

It was not at all what I had intended, but I forced myself to feel grateful. I could see no other way.

By the time I got back to Pikersfield Manor that evening, I never wanted to see another strawberry ever again. The fruit farm paid cash according to weight picked, so we picked at a furious rate all afternoon, toiling under a hot sun while the horses dozed, tied to a fence in the shade. Ginny and Rich took Tess back to Swallowbridge with them, so I had to catch a bus to Pikersfield. I was late home, my back ached agonizingly and, in all the urgency of needing to get hold of enough hard cash to buy the gray

46

when his owner was found, I had completely forgotten my promise to Melissa.

"Goodness, you ain't never seen fireworks like it, when you didn't turn up!" Mrs. Poppy reported, slapping her rolling pin across some pastry. "Madam Melissa was REAL steamed up. Said you promised, cross your heart, to come back and tell her all about some old horse. Boiling up for another of her bad turns, she was, until your mom said she'd take her for a drive. But it will take more than a spin in a motor to sweeten Melissa, I'll be bound. I'd make myself scarce, if I was you. Your mom is right cross with you. I'll have a shot at calming her down when she gets back."

Munching one of Mrs. Poppy's freshly baked pastries and cursing myself for being an idiot, I took her advice and fled the house. I was in trouble again and, yet again, it was all my fault. I should have phoned Melissa to tell her what had happened. My mother would be in no mood, now, to give a sympathetic ear to the story of the gray and, because I had upset her, Melissa might have decided against the idea of asking her father to allow Tess to come to Pikersfield Manor. Perhaps Ginny was right about there being too many ifs and buts.

I wandered into the yard, looked around at all those stables and told myself not to give up so easily. There would be no harm in exploring the stables. I would need to be well organized, just in case everything worked out alright in the end.

I knew already that all the outer doors were locked, but I rattled a few, just to make sure. The hinges were strong and the padlocks held. I circled the yard. Only the garages were open. They ran in a row from the gate arch to the lower, left-hand corner of the yard, where the garage that housed Mom's car joined the newest stable wing. I glanced in at the space where the old estate car usually stood – and I had found it at last: a way in. A door led from inside the garage to the internal walkway that stretched the length of the left-hand stable block.

I caught my breath in excitement. Melissa had described it as a "horsy palace" and she was right. The walkway led past six spectacular loose boxes. No expense had been spared, from the pale blue tiles that lined every box above the kicking boards, to the bluestone cobbled floor with its efficient drainage system. The tall windows and double doors, on the yard side of the walkway, would make the building light and airy when they were cleaned and opened. At the far end of the block, a feed store and a tack room were fitted out with bins, racks, and water taps that still worked. With no more than a spring clean, Tess and the gray would have a magnificent home.

More out of curiosity than a need to discover any more stables, I turned the corner at the end of the walkway and found myself in the wing at the back of the yard. Here the loose boxes were less grand but just as serviceable, with grill-topped, wooden partitions that curved down from the back wall to pillars at the front, each crowned with a hand-somely carved finial. At this rate, Tess and the gray would be spoiled for sure! In this wing, too, the internal walkway stretched the length of the block, with several doors and windows on its yard side. I turned the final corner and was in the oldest stable block of all. The building was full of rubbish.

I peered into the gloom and could see nothing but heaps of junk. The long, low building had, at some time, been divided into stalls by rough wooden partitions but, since then, it had become a dumping place for years worth of household rubbish. To make more room for the moldering trunks, broken furniture, rusted lawn mowers, and the rest of the mess, the partitions had been smashed from their places and stacked against the wall at the far end.

My curiosity satisfied, I was turning to leave when I heard a noise. I froze, my ears straining to catch the sound in the rustling shadows. It was a long way back through the buildings to the garage escape route and, suddenly, I remembered Melissa's tale of the stable ghost. I was poised to run, the hair prickling with fear on my scalp. The sound came again, a scratching, scuffling, pattering, and then a distinct meow. I relaxed and felt silly. It was only a cat.

A little, tortoise-shell colored "she-cat", very ordinary and un-ghostlike, popped from behind a box and began to weave about round my legs. Three kittens clambered over the rubbish behind their mother. They were enchanting and very friendly. I knelt on the dusty floor to stroke them, while the mother cat pushed onto my lap and purred. I couldn't think what the cats were doing there. They were far too tame to be feral, and too well fed and healthy to be strays.

The kittens were too lively to sit still for long. They began to play, chasing and tumbling away down the building until, all of a sudden, they vanished. Their mother followed them, apparently straight through the wall. I picked my way round the junk to the far end, and peered behind the stacked wooden partitions. There was no sign of the cats, but I could hear them moving about on the other side of what should have been the end wall of the block.

Puzzled, I retraced my steps, counting windows as I went. There were five windows in this wing, two on one side and three on the other of the locked outer door. I sprinted back round the corner, along the middle wing walkway, round the next corner, down the length of the

49

new wing and out of the garage. I stood in the yard and counted windows again. Still there were five. But then I saw, partly concealed by the ivy that festooned the gable end, right at the end of the oldest wing of the stable block, the unmistakable evidence that a sixth window had been bricked-up. Behind it must be the space into which the cats had vanished – a hidden room.

"Oh, that's Muff. Pretty little cat, isn't she?" Mrs. Poppy was putting on her coat and about to go home when I rushed into the kitchen, asking about kittens and looking for a torch. Mom and Melissa were not yet back. "I gave Muff to Melissa, a while gone. Thought a pet would cheer her up, but I soon got my head bitten off, didn't I? It brings Madam up in a rash, cat's fur does, so the poor little thing got kicked out of the house. I usually feed them cats on my way home, so you can save me a job if you like."

Used to being fed at the same time every evening, the cats were waiting in the garage when I returned to the yard. I put down their dishes of cat food and milk, made a fuss of them again, then trotted all the way round the insides of the stable wings to the rubbish filled gloom of the oldest block. By now dusk was deepening the shadows, but Mrs. Poppy's torch was a large one with strong batteries.

It took me ages to shift the heavy stall partitions from the end wall, and I was sweating and panting by the time the last one crashed to the side. Behind it was a door. It looked very old, made of oak studded with iron nails and sagging on its enormous, rusted hinges. The bottom of the door had rotted with time, and traces of cat's fur on the crumbling corner showed where Muff and her kittens had squeezed through. The stiff latch refused to budge until I walloped it with my shoe, then the door at last groaned open.

I was not sure what I was expecting to find, but I was bitterly disappointed when the swinging torch beam revealed nothing but an empty room. Worm-eaten, wooden saddle racks and bridle brackets told me that it must once have been a tack room, but it was a tack room stripped bare, abandoned and of no interest to anyone. All my hard work had been for nothing.

From what Melissa had told me, I knew that it had been her great, great grandfather who had built himself another block of stables and abandoned this one to become, eventually, no more than a rubbish dump. If, in his exasperation at failing to lay the ghost, he had not cared what happened to the rest of the building, WHY had he so carefully sealed up and hidden this empty room? Why had he gone to the trouble of bricking up the window and blocking the doorway, instead of leaving it, like the rest, as a dumping place?

By now my eyes had adjusted to the gloom, and I realized that the room was not completely empty after all. On one of the racks something bulky was swathed in dusty cloths. I put the torch on the floor and, rather gingerly, pulled aside a fold of the material. It felt like silk and it was greasy, as if it had been oiled to protect something from damp and dirt. Beneath the wrappings was a leather cover. When I removed the cover and picked up the torch, I was quite unprepared for the beauty of blue and gold that blazed into life in front of me.

It had to be a saddle, but was quite unlike any saddle I had ever seen before. The seat looked more like a plump, square cushion than a saddle, and was of dark blue velvet, bordered round with a fringe of gold tassels. Down either side, instead of saddle flaps, hung long panels of blue velvet richly worked with a geometric design of embroidery, padded and raised with gold thread. It had one raised pommel, as if it was a ladies saddle, but no leaping head or stir-rup fixing like a modern sidesaddle. The whole thing was exquisitely beautiful and very, very old.

I hardly dared to touch it, but I couldn't resist running one finger lightly over the embroidery, admiring the skill of the workmanship. The velvet was still surprisingly sound although, rather touchingly, the seat was, in places, worn threadbare with much use. I wondered whom she had been, the fine lady of long ago who had owned such a gorgeous saddle and so much loved to ride.

And then the sobbing began.

The air above my head quivered with the sound of a girl's voice crying her misery and utter desolation.

"Who's there?" I called sharply. "Is someone there?" But the sobbing went on and on without pause. It had been a stupid question. I knew I was alone in the building, and how could there be anything human in the empty air above me?

Oddly enough, I was not frightened. The voice held no menace or terror, just a sadness so intense that it swamped me, driving out all emotion other than a shared wretched-ness. Tears filled my eyes, and I couldn't help but sob in sympathy with the unseen sufferer.

The sound of crying continued for several minutes, then ceased. The tap of light footsteps seemed to come down from the ceiling of the room, pass close to me, and echo away through the building until they faded into silence. I was trembling now; from shock, from the intensity of what I had just heard, and from the awful anguish that I had been forced to share with someone who wasn't even there.

My hands shook as I shone the torch in a slow arc across the ceiling. Now I knew why Melissa's great, great grand-father had hidden this room. He had shut it away because it was the place in which the legend of the Wailing Woman of Pikersfield had its origins. I was sure that, somewhere above my head, the reason for her existence might be found.

The voice had come from the roof space above the hidden tack room. I examined the ceiling closely. Its plaster was falling apart in places and its whole surface was crazed with cracks, but there was no sign of a trap door, nor any outline that might indicate a concealed entrance. I went back through the old door and shined my torch again at the roof.

There was no plaster ceiling here, above the area once occupied by stalls. Instead, over my head, there were just rotten boards with gaps between them that revealed dark space beyond. It took me a while to pick my way through the rubbish, to realize that there was a hayloft above with traps in its floor, at intervals along the back, through which fodder had once been tedded to the stalls below. I made a precarious heap of boxes, and climbed to raise my head through one of the traps.

I had drawn another blank. The loft was empty and the torch light reflected back from the brick triangle of the gable at the hidden tack room end of the building. I ducked down to shine the torch towards the tack room door, then reached up through the trap again, and shined it at the gable end. Up, down, several times and then I was almost sure. Distances can be deceptive, especially in inky darkness with nothing but torchlight to go by, and I would have to do some measuring in daylight to be certain, but it seemed to me that the hayloft above must be several feet shorter than the building below. That brick triangle was not the gable end at all!

Thoughtfully, I returned to the tack room and re-packed the blue and gold sidesaddle in the leather cover and oiled cloth that had preserved it for so long. Above my head, I knew, was a concealed space in the roof void, and I was determined to find a way in. I could not understand why I felt such determination, I just did and I couldn't help it. Perhaps it was yet another trick the House of Tears was playing on me.

"House of Tears," I repeated to the dusty, cobwebbed darkness, and it brought back Mr. Poppy's mysterious ramblings about time coming full circle to bring the tears to an end. Was that why the house had felt as if it was expecting me? If so, what else did Mr. Poppy know that he had not told me? I had been mistaken when I assumed he was talking about Melissa. They were not her tears he meant, but the tears of the Wailing Woman of Pikersfield.

Chapter Six

I had been able to laugh at Melissa's story of the Wailing Woman, and to dismiss it as no more than a folk legend, because it had been my choice whether to believe it or not. Now that I had heard the sobbing voice for myself, I had no choice in the matter: I was compelled to believe that the ghost existed. Not only that, but I had the uncomfortable conviction that I was fated to become mixed up with her, whoever she was, whether I liked it or not.

I knew I could share my secret with no one. Who would believe me anyway? One person alone would understand, and I must talk to Mr. Poppy as soon as possible. After that, with or without his help, I must find a way into the roof above the hidden tack room, and search for an answer to the mystery of the ghostly voice. As it turned out, a series of calamities delayed my plans.

My mother was furious. She had been annoyed when I failed to return that afternoon to sit with Melissa. Her annoyance had deepened to anger when she heard, from Melissa of course, of my broken promise that nearly triggered another of the girl's attacks. When she and Melissa came home from their drive to find me still absent, and then it was very late in the evening before I finally turned up, Mom erupted into a fury so out of character that it scared me.

To make matters worse, I couldn't tell Mom about the hidden tack room and the sobbing voice, so I had to say I had just been wandering about, which was a pretty feeble excuse and held no weight with Mom. My mind totally distracted by the ghost, I blurted out the story of the gray, my urgent need to rescue him, and the consequent fruit picking job, without giving any thought to tactful phrasing. It seemed that I was digging a deeper and deeper pit of trouble for myself, and I was helpless to do anything about it.

"Melissa isn't a BABY!" I yelled in desperation at Mom. "I told her all about the gray, and she said she really cared about what happened to him, so she's bound to understand why I couldn't get back. I got along really well with her last night."

"All the more reason to keep your promise to her today," Mom replied coldly. "Don't you realize how fragile her emotions have become, after being let down so often? Honestly Anna, I gave you credit for having more sense! It's no use winning Melissa's trust, and then forgetting all about her to go off on some fool's errand to rescue a horse that has nothing to do with you. Melissa is a very sick little girl. She is weak and in pain. I'm amazed that you can be so unfeeling and selfish! I'm disappointed in you, Anna, I am, really."

I knew it could be useless to tell my mother of my suspicions regarding Melissa. I suspected that Melissa's asthma attacks were mainly self-induced, I was fairly sure that her leg hurt only when it suited her, and I was certain that somebody who could tuck away three cheeseburgers and two ice-cream sundaes in one sitting would be far from weak. Not only was my mother too angry to listen, but she was so worried by the burden of her responsibility for the invalid, that I would only antagonize her the more by saying such things.

"Pull yourself together, Anna, and try to behave more like a responsible adult." Mom lectured me. "You will not buy another horse. Leave rescuing horses to the ASPCA, it's their job. You may go fruit picking, but *only* because it will do you good to earn your own pocket money, and *only* in the afternoons. I can't be with Melissa every hour of the day, I'm responsible for the running of this big house as well, so you will keep your promise to Melissa and sit with her every morning."

That my mother should take Melissa's side so completely, and that she should think so very badly of me, made me sick at heart. But I could not blame her for it because, over the next few days, I came to understand why – my gentle, tender-hearted, loving, gullible mother was being totally deceived by an expert.

Whenever Mom was around, Melissa was always polite, obedient, even affectionate. She limped, she sighed, and she pathetically refused food. She was the picture of a model patient bravely bearing great pain and unhappiness with fortitude. Melissa had been practicing getting her own way and everybody's attention by feigned illness for so long that, by now, her act was foolproof. The only difference was that whereas Melissa seemed to hate everyone else, she adored my mother. With the rudeness that had alienated people like Mrs. Poppy removed from the act, my mother was completely under its spell.

The real Melissa emerged only when my mother was not there to see her. When I was alone with her during those long, devious, horrible mornings, Melissa reverted to being every bit as unpleasant as she had been my first evening at

Pikersfield Manor. Only now she had discovered the amusing new pastime of driving a wedge between me and my mother. It was as if, having at last found someone who unreservedly loved her, Melissa needed to keep that person all to herself. I had the nasty feeling that Melissa Hyde-Grant was trying to take my mother away from me.

"How is the horse rescue going?" Melissa asked me, one morning. I was sitting on her bedroom window seat and longing to be outside in the fresh air. Ginny and Rich were looking after the gray horse and doing the lion's share of the fruit picking. At this rate the horse would end up belonging more to them than to me.

"Well, how is it going?" she repeated. "Have you made enough money to buy him yet?"

I fell into her trap.

"Not really. We've earned quite a bit between us and the ASPCA haven't yet managed to trace his owner, so we still have time to earn more. I'm just keeping my fingers crossed. I couldn't bear to lose him now!"

"I knew it!" Melissa gloated her triumph. "I KNEW you still meant to buy him, even after your mother said you were not to. You just wait till I tell her."

"You wouldn't!"

"Just watch me!" Melissa gave me a nasty grin and I knew she would.

"He will belong to Ginny and Rich as well," I hastened to explain.

"Same difference. AND I'll tell her you've broken your promise to teach me to ride. AND I'll tell her you've been poking about in the stable yard, early in the morning, planning to bring Tess and the gray horse here without even asking."

"That is a complete lie!"

"Oh no it isn't, because I've seen you from the east wing landing window."

I had, in fact, been in the stable yard very early that morning, long before even Mom was awake. I had been doing the measuring that proved that the hayloft above the old stable wing came to a dead, bricked-up end some 12 feet before the end wall of the ground floor. Then I had been assembling and hiding the ladder and tools I would need to break through the ceiling of the hidden tack room, to find the unaccounted for space in the roof above it. But, if I wanted to keep it a secret, there was no way I could tell Melissa what I had been doing. The best form of defense was attack. It was quite a distance from Melissa's bedroom to the housekeeper's landing at the back of the house.

"So, you CAN manage to stagger THAT far to spy on me, can you? I suppose you also managed a quick trip to the kitchen, to gobble up enough food so you could refuse your breakfast and be all weak and pathetic, then my poor mother will spend all day worrying about you. Are you going to tell her that too?"

Melissa gave me such a venomous look that I was surprised it didn't curl the wallpaper. "I won't tell her anything if you let me ride Tess."

"That's blackmail! Anyway, I wouldn't dare to let you ride anything, unless I had your father's permission. Our bargain was that you would write to ask him first."

"I did. He said YES: Yes, yes, yes! So, what about tomorrow morning?"

This threw me somewhat, but I was excited. Tess was a hoof nearer moving to Pikersfield after all, only it was funny that my mother hadn't told me so. Or was it? She was still very cool and disapproving towards me. Besides which, we saw little of each other these days. Mom was busy every morning while I sat with Melissa, and I was out until late every afternoon, fruit picking. Mom had gone shopping this morning, and she planned to visit a friend in Chawton tomorrow morning.

I gazed out of the window, across the sun-washed lavender of the terrace to the knot garden, and wondered what to do. Mr. Poppy was bent over his herbs. I hadn't seen him since my brush with the Wailing Woman, and I desperately needed to talk to him. I began to lose patience with Melissa and her devious ways. So far Melissa had brought me only grief and trouble, and the prospect of introducing Madam Trouble to ponies boded all manner of consequences too awful to contemplate. But, if I refused, Mom would accuse me of yet another broken promise, and if I wanted Tess here with me, then I had no choice. Mr. Poppy looked to be packing up his tools. I would have to be quick to catch him.

"I think it would be best to wait until Mom can be here for your first ride, just in case the horse hair brings on one of your attacks." I stood up, my eyes still on the bent form of the gardener, and I hoped to put Melissa off for a while.

"I'll tell her today. I'll have my inhaler and I can take one of my pills. And if your mother thinks she ought to be here, then she'll stay at home, wont she?"

Oh yes, I thought bitterly, of course she would. Mom would do anything for Melissa.

"Tomorrow morning then," Melissa ordered, as I left the room. "You WILL give me my first riding lesson tomorrow morning!"

Mr. Poppy seemed to give little attention to much else in the unkempt gardens save the knot garden but, for all his work, the fragrant plants continued to defy the confines of their ancient, hedge-lined maze of beds. Perhaps he couldn't bear to cut them back, except for taking just enough to make the bunches of herbs that dried above the kitchen stove. I had developed a taste for Mrs. Poppy's chamomile tea.

Already I knew how to get the old man on my side. "How is your back, Mr. Poppy," I asked.

"Middling fair." He straightened up, giving me a wary look. "You're still here then? I thought you'd have been frightened off by now. You've been going places you have no business to go. Happen you've learned your lesson."

"All I have learned, Mr. Poppy, is what you meant by the House of Tears, and it has nothing to do with Melissa. You should have told me the truth. You should have warned me because you know, don't you?"

"I know nothing except that I heard her again the other night, same as you did, what set her off. She's best left alone. The Old Master, him that's been gone these many, many years, he knew it too. The Old Master and my great grandfather shut her away. It was the best thing to do then, and 'tis the best thing to do now."

"Who is she, Mr. Poppy?" I asked, urgently. "Where is she? I know I've got to find her, the house knows I'm meant to find her, but how and where, and then what am I supposed to do? You said that time has come full circle and it's time for the tears to end – what did you mean?"

"You surely ask a pother of questions, blest if I can remember the answers!" Mr. Poppy pulled a spotted handkerchief from his pocket and mopped his forehead, then turned away from me. Infuriated, I looked around to find a way to get his attention. My gaze fell on a bush of the spiky little leaves that my mother cooked with lamb. I had been reading "Hamlet" at school, and Ophelia's words came unbidden to my lips.

"There's rosemary, that's for remembrance!" I plucked a handful of the plant and thrust it under Mr. Poppy's nose. Commanded by one of his beloved herbs, the old man's hostility vanished. He crushed the leaves between his palms, and took a few faltering steps to subside onto the terrace wall. I sat beside him and waited.

"And rue for the pain of remembering," he said, at length, "and 'tis a great pain to me because I don't remember all. Time was when every place had its folk memory, handed down not just in legends by the people, but by the very earth and stones of the place. In those days people stayed put, generation after generation in one place, never going far from their villages. 'Tis not the same now, with your cars and planes, telephones, and television, and all the rest that goes to make the world seem so small that families are split across the globe and think nothing of it. The folk memory has been destroyed, and with it has gone the ancient wisdom. Even where the earth and stones remember still, their voices are being buried under acres of concrete and new estates, where strangers have no ears to hear. Only in rare places now, such as this old House of Tears, can the echoes from the past make themselves heard, and only rarely can people hear them. Folks don't believe in ghosts no more, you see?"

The old man sat on the wall, his gnarled hands resting on the top of his spade and his rheumy eyes gazing into the distance. The sun was hot on our faces, and the rich scents of the knot garden were strong in our nostrils.

"Even when I were a nipper the folk memory had faded," Mr. Poppy said sadly. "I heard the words, but I can't recall the meaning, try as I might. She cries, but they never said why. Folks hereabouts knew, once upon a time, but the knowledge is lost now, and with it the wisdom of the remedy."

The old man chuckled, but without mirth. This time I could make sense of his riddles. All he was saying was that he had no help to give me.

"No, I can't help you, Anna Hurst, you are on your own in this business. But there is one thing I do recall of the legend. It was said that, when time has come full circle and the right people are gathered together, the tears will be brought to an end and the old house will be released from the thrall of its past. Perhaps you will be the one to bring it about, but you will not do it by yourself. Only blood can free blood, only family can release family, only the love of kin for kin can bring an end to this particular curse of unrest."

Mr. Poppy rose stiffly to his feet and hobbled away, leaving me very little the wiser. If answers there were to be found, there was only the one place I would find them: the lost space above the hidden room.

Chapter Seven

Even at such short notice, Melissa's riding lesson was fairly easy to organize. I talked it over with Ginny and Rich during our afternoon fruit picking session, and we arranged that they would ride to Pikersfield manor the next morning, leading Tess. Melissa would use Tess for her lesson in the orchard, and then I would ride Tess to work in the afternoon with the others. Ginny was not keen on the idea. I pointed out that, if all went well, it would take only a few rides for Melissa to persuade Mr. Hyde-Grant and my mother of the sense of Tess staying permanently at the manor. Ginny agreed, reluctantly, but said it was only to oblige me. Obliging people like Melissa, she stated, was not in her nature.

I was up early again the next morning, and spent ages slashing with a hook at the long grass in the orchard. It took me far longer than I expected to clear a schooling area that was free from both scrub and overhanging branches, and when I returned to the house Mom was already leaving to visit her friend in Chawton.

"Are you going anyway?" I asked in amazement. "I was sure you would want to keep an eye on Melissa this morning, just in case anything goes wrong."

"Why should it? I'm sure you have learned your lesson

by now, and you should be quite capable of looking after Melissa. Just remember to keep her inhaler handy and don't let her overdo things."

I was very relieved to see that Mom had, at last, thawed out towards me enough to trust me. I knew that it would please Mom if Melissa found a new interest to keep her busy and happy out of doors, instead of moping in her room all day. Mom's relief and pleasure would bridge the gap between us, ending the estrangement that I found so hard to bear. Nevertheless, I was greatly surprised when Mom drove away without giving me a string of anxious instructions, or even a backward glance.

The horses had a magical effect on Melissa. She waited at the orchard gate, hopping from foot to foot with excitement, until they turned into the drive. Then she ran to meet them and patted each in turn, almost speechless with joy. She was not intimidated by the size of Mr. Big, she thought that Tess' black and white markings were gorgeous, and she told Ginny that she must be an amazingly good rider to cope with Pearly. Pearly was one of those hot ponies that have a mental block about standing still and do a lot of prancing about. The direct route to Ginny's heart was to admire Pearly, so the rather poker-faced expression with which Ginny had arrived softened considerably.

Melissa's bad leg did not make her beginner's awkwardness noticeably worse and, although she became a little runny-eyed and sniffly, the horse hair did not affect her badly. Very soon she was wearing my riding hat and in the saddle, walking Tess round the cleared area in the orchard. Rich walked at Tess' head holding the lead rope, while I stood in the middle and called out all the usual things such as heels down, elbows in and try not to jab at Tess' mouth.

"Well I'm blown away, she catches on quickly," Ginny

remarked. "I'm surprised she's got such a good sense of balance, seeing as she spends her life lying around doing nothing but whine!"

Ginny was right. Melissa seemed to have a natural aptitude for riding. Within half an hour, she was doing halt to walk and walk to halt, circling on both reins, sitting correctly and keeping her hands in a good position with a nice feel on the reins. I was proud of my pupil and told her so. Melissa blushed with pleasure.

"Please may I try a trot now, Anna?"

"Better ask Rich, he's doing the running beside. But only if you are not feeling tired."

"Rich, can we trot please?"

"Check that out!" Ginny exclaimed, as Melissa bumped away across the grass. "All these pleases and thank yous and generally being nice. You'll have to stick her on a horse more often, for everyone's sake."

Rich was singing out, "Up, down, up, down," as Melissa very quickly got the hang of rising trot.

"I think that's enough for today," I said, when Melissa had managed a whole circuit without bumping on the wrong stride. She was looking hot and breathless, as was Tess, who had covered several miles even before the lesson began. "We'll do a few mounts and dismounts, then give Tess a rest."

"I'm not tired. I don't want to get off. I want to canter." Melissa sounded mutinous.

"I knew it was too good to last!" Ginny muttered.

"Next time," I promised. "Tess has had enough, and you'll be horribly stiff tomorrow if you do too much the first time."

"I WANT to canter NOW!" Melissa jerked on the rein and yanked Tess' head to one side. Rich grabbed for the bit to hold her back. Tess, caught in the middle of a tug of war, flattened her ears and rolled her eyes,

"Stop behaving like a spoiled brat, Melissa," Ginny bawled. "The pony needs a rest, then we've got to get off to work."

"How dare you call me names!" Melissa shrieked. She booted Tess hard in the ribs and Tess, already upset by the shouting and rough treatment, shot forward.

Rich was caught off balance by Tess' barging shoulder. He stumbled to his knees and let go of the lead rope. Melissa's heels kept pummeling but, in the excitement of cantering, she forgot to steer, so Tess veered off the cleared circle and careered away into the long grass, heading for the gate and escape. She caught her hoof in a trailing bramble, pitched violently forwards, then regained her balance with a plunge, a heave, and an infuriated buck. Melissa was hurled from the saddle and hit the ground with a thump.

I sprinted across the orchard, cursing Ginny's sharp tongue for upsetting Melissa just when everything was going so well.

"Come on, up you get Melissa," I said, trying to sound breezy and encouraging. "Everyone has to fall off sooner or later, and they say it takes seven falls before you can call yourself a rider!"

But Melissa just lay there, screaming and screaming and screaming.

"My back, my back," she screamed. "You've broken my back. I can't move my legs." Then the dreaded wheezing began, and Melissa was fighting for her breath.

We were Pony Club trained, so we knew what to do and did it at once. Rich ran to phone for an ambulance, while Ginny and I put our rolled coats against Melissa's sides to keep her still, and covered her to keep her warm. With a possible spinal injury it was essential not to move her, not even to take off her hat.

"At least we won't have to give her the kiss of life!" Ginny said, with scant evidence of sympathy. "There can't be much wrong with her airway if she can scream like that. Oh do shut up, Melissa, it can't be that bad."

I silenced Ginny with a glare and Melissa by slipping her inhaler between her lips. I prayed that the ambulance would arrive before her asthma attack, really got going. I felt physically sick with worry. Melissa might be seriously hurt and my mother was bound to blame me.

I spent the rest of that day and most of the night in the waiting room of Chawton Hospital casualty department. By dawn I hated the place! My mother arrived at the hospital within minutes of my phone call to her friend's house and, after consultation with the doctor, she sent an urgent message to Oxford, summoning Mr. Hyde-Grant to come at once.

I waited on my own for hours. Mom and Mr. Hyde-Grant were with Melissa while first one doctor, then another, then a specialist examined her, and she had a series of tests and X-rays. It was not until they came to collect me to return to the Manor, that I was able to explain how the accident had happened. Only then did I realize the full enormity of the situation: Melissa had tricked me.

Melissa had never written to her father. Melissa had made no mention whatsoever of the riding lesson to my mother. Neither of them knew a thing about it and, had they done so, they would have forbidden it anyway. I should have double-checked, instead of taking Melissa at her word. It had all happened in such a hurry and I had been distracted, first by my need to talk to Mr. Poppy and then by the time it took to clear the grass in the orchard, but that was no excuse. As usual, I had only myself to blame.

"Honestly, I thought you both knew." My voice shook with my desperation to make Mom and Mr. Hyde-Grant believe me. "Melissa told me that she had asked both of you and that it was alright!"

"Use your intelligence, Anna!" Mom raged. "Would I have gone out and left such a crazy scheme unsupervised? Would I have ever agreed to it in the first place? How could you be so stupid and irresponsible?"

"How was I to know Melissa was lying?" I pleaded. "Of course I was surprised when you went out. Didn't I say to you that I thought you would want to keep an eye on Melissa? Don't you remember?"

"Yes, I remember." My poor mother was looking upset and confused. "And I believe you, Anna. The one thing I am sure of is that you always tell the truth. But if Melissa did play such a trick on you, why? It just doesn't make sense."

Given that Melissa thoroughly enjoyed dumping me in hot water, it made a great deal of sense to me, but I couldn't say so because it would make me look petty and childish and no one would believe it anyway. Mr. Hyde-Grant was skeptical but prepared to accept my word. He seemed impatient to get away and, as far as Melissa was concerned, out of sight was out of mind. Now that the emergency was over, he couldn't be bothered with post mortems or arguments.

So I was to be blamed for no more than a lack of intelligence and I had been forgiven for that, but I felt it was only with reservations and on sufferance. I hoped that Melissa would at least have the decency to tell the truth and clear my name, but no such luck. She claimed that she could remember nothing about the accident, but was sure that she had never asked to ride Tess. "I would never be so silly," she whispered pathetically to Mom. "I know horse hair makes me ill, so I can never have fun like normal children!"

The doctors could find nothing physically wrong with Melissa, although they kept her in hospital overnight for observation. Unfortunately, when Melissa came home she insisted that her legs wouldn't work properly and she could hardly walk, so another doctor was summoned. He gave Mom a long lecture about shock, post-accident trauma and psychosomatic illness.

"The poor girl suffered a dreadful shock to the system," he said. "She will need time and a great deal of professional care to get over it. There is probably some psychological reason why she is frightened to walk, but psychosomatic illness is every bit as real a physical injury. I think that counseling by a child psychologist would be a good idea."

For my part, I thought that strangling the poor little girl would be a good idea. Mr. Hyde-Grant went back to Oxford the same day that Melissa was discharged from hospital, leaving my mother to cope on her own with the fractious, bed-ridden invalid. I needed a shoulder to cry on, but had no one to share my miseries except for the gray horse and my long-suffering friends.

I leaned on the paddock gate and watched the gray horse kick up his heels in the sunshine. He was still thin, but his coat was clean and beginning to take on the gloss of returning health, and he was showing a renewed interest in life with a buck, a squeal, and a canter round his field. When he had finished letting off steam, he came to the gate and pushed his muzzle into my hand, seeking attention. Rich had taken charge of the fruit picking money and his cash box was filling up fast. The three of us already regarded the gray horse as practically our own property.

"I wonder what he's like to ride?" Ginny mused.

"There's only one way to find out," I said. "Rich, can I borrow Big's tack?"

"Do you think that's wise, he might not even be broken in," Rich warned.

"Bound to be by his age. Anyway, I'll be careful and it will soon be pretty obvious if he isn't." I had looked at the gray's teeth and decided that he was about 8 years old. His action, as he stretched his legs round the paddock, was impressive and, like Ginny, I was longing to find out what he felt like under saddle.

"I suppose you're right," Rich relented, "and it's just as well to discover exactly what we are buying, in case he's a rogue. He might have been dumped here because he's dangerous, or has some awful vice."

Rich's warning made me extra careful, but I was sure that the gray was no rogue. I was getting a very special feeling about this horse. I adjusted Big's tack to fit the gray, and he accepted the bit willingly and took no notice when I tightened the girth – both good signs. I pushed to the back of my mind the future problem of finding the money for new tack, even though I knew that little Tess' saddle and bridle would be no use at all for the tall horse.

First, I put both my arms across his back and leaned my chest against the saddle. The gray took no notice. Then Rich gave me a leg up, so that I was lying with my full weight over his withers. The gray stood like a rock. Slowly and cautiously, I swung one leg over the saddle and sat up.

"Told you so!" I grinned, but Ginny and Rich walked at the gray's head for a circuit of the paddock, just in case I

71

was wrong. By then I was sure it was safe to put my feet in the stirrups and take up a contact with the reins.

It quickly became apparent that not only had the gray been broken to ride but, at some time in his life, he had been expertly schooled. His responses to the aids were a little ragged, and he would need some reminding and re-schooling, but he still felt fantastic to ride. He dropped his nose obediently to the snaffle bit and moved with a long, floating stride that felt very different from ponyish little Tess. He arched his neck and flipped his toes when I asked him to trot, and when I cantered him in a figure of eight, we managed a passable flying change in the middle.

"Boy oh boy, what a find!" Rich exclaimed. "Most people have to search for ages before they come across a horse like this, and here he is, more or less handed to us on a plate."

"Wow!" Ginny breathed in awe. "I never dreamed I'd be part owner of such a class horse! What a mover! But if his owner knows anything at all about horses, we'll never be able to afford his asking price. Maybe we ought to scruff the horse up again."

"I didn't hear that!" Peter Sams was watching us over the gate and laughing.

"We thought you'd forgotten us," Ginny accused.

"Could I ever? You're trespassing again, and I've got some news for you."

I untacked the gray and turned him loose. For once he did not ravenously attack his hay, but stayed by the gate and rested his head on my shoulder. He seemed to have sin-gled me out as his special human and, already, I felt fierce-ly possessive about him.

"I don't know where his owner is," Mr. Sams told us, "but I almost know who he is. He is a man who used to live on the Pikersfield estate. He bought the gray just before last Christmas, as a present for his wife. He didn't know a thing about horses himself and when his wife walked out on him, shortly afterwards, it seems he abandoned the horse to fend for itself. He rented this bit of ground from a farmer who lives in Winterford and doesn't come here often. The horse's owner hasn't paid the rent for months, and the farmer didn't realize the horse was still here. Anyway, the owner moved away from Pikersfield in February. His friends on the estate have promised to contact him, so all I can do now is wait to hear from him."

"Didn't they give you his name and new address?" Rich asked.

"I tried to get it out of them, but they were too smart for that – probably realize there might be a prosecution for cruelty involved! The owner might never show up, or…"

"Or what?" Ginny demanded.

"Well, that's the worry. Or the owner might sneak back and spirit the horse away when no one is looking, then there is no evidence and no one to prosecute. I've known it to happen before. If you see a stranger hanging about, let me know. Here's the number of my cell phone, get hold of me any time. Meanwhile, I'll do something about getting the horse shifted to a safer place."

Rich tucked the inspector's card into his pocket, and we watched the white van drive away.

"That's worse than not knowing," Ginny said gloomily.

"And we can't watch him 24 hours a day," I agreed. "Especially not at night, which is the most obvious time for spiriting things away."

"If we had enough people we could set up a rota," Rich said. "It won't be for long, if Mr. Sams is going to take him away fairly soon. I know my dad will run me over in the car for a late night check tonight, then there's Charlie and Cathy, and all the other liveries at the Rectory."

"Right, let's get weaving!" As was usual when she got her teeth into something, Ginny wanted everything done yesterday. She was already tightening Pearly's girth and reeling off the names of people who might help. Once she got hold of them, they would have little chance to say no.

"Do you mind if I leave the organizing to you?" I asked. "There is something I've got to do at home."

"Of course, you'll have your work cut out looking after Melissa," Rich said. "How is she?

""Much the same. I think her legs would walk but her mind won't let them."

"Set fire to the bed, that would soon shift her," Ginny suggested.

I shook my head grimly. "No, apparently psychosomatic illness is not as simple as that. Mom and the doctor think she ought to see a psychologist, but Mr. Hyde-Grant won't hear of it."

"Don't worry, we'll see to the gray," Rich said, "and we'll do your share of the fruit picking this afternoon."

"Yet again!" Ginny remarked, but I knew it was without rancor. She was inclined to say some pretty heartless things about Melissa, but only because she thought Melissa was making life very difficult for me. Ginny was a fiercely loyal friend and, as far as Melissa was concerned, she was right.

Chapter Eight

The stable yard behind Pikersfield Manor House was deserted except for muff and her kittens, who were sprawled on the cobbles, dozing in the sun. It was Mrs. Poppy's day off, Mr. Poppy's back was playing him up again and my mother would be with Melissa all afternoon. I was not needed in the sickroom but had been happy for Ginny and Rich to think that I was, because this was the perfect opportunity to investigate the roof above the hidden tack room. I knew I would have several hours without fear of discovery or interruption. I lugged the pair of steps, torch and tools all the way around the insides of the stable blocks into the secret room, and wedged the door shut behind me.

With the door closed and the window bricked-up, the room was pitch dark. I had to carry the torch the whole time, as I moved the steps inch by tedious inch across the floor, climbing endlessly up and down to probe the ceiling above my head with a screwdriver. Flakes of lime wash and pieces of ancient plaster, bonded with tufts of equally ancient horse hair, pattered onto my shoulders and gritted into my eyes. The ladder and the torch seemed to get heavier by the minute, until they weighed a ton. My arms ached and the dust made me cough. I found nothing.

I worked my way methodically around the entire area of

the ceiling and, as I moved the steps under the very last section in the far corner of the room, I'd just about had enough of it. Maybe I was wrong. Obviously there was no trap door, no plastered over, cunningly concealed entrance into the roof void above. Where the screwdriver penetrated the plaster it met resistance, not empty space. In the places where plaster, lathes and all had fallen away from the ceiling, there was solid, age-hardened timber above the joists and no way through.

By now my arms were in agony from so much reaching above my head, and I sat on the top step of the ladder, almost crying from exhaustion and frustration. After all, what clues could a ghost possibly leave for me to find? The sobbing had been no more than a voice, and the light footsteps had passed right beside me but I had seen nothing. "Oh c'mon!" I yelled, and flung the screwdriver at the wall. It hit the boards with a hollow thud.

I was down the steps in an instant, excited and no longer tired. I had only just registered the fact that only the back wall was boarded, lined with rough planks like a primitive paneling – why just the one wall of the room? I began at the other end, tapping along the boards with a hammer until I reached the place where the screwdriver had hit the wall. The flat sounding taps changed to hollow thuds with a faint echo reverberating behind them. There was no outline to suggest a door, but I felt along the planks, pushing and testing each in turn.

It happened so suddenly that I was taken by surprise and almost fell through the opening. A section of the woodwork had pivoted on its own axis, and turned inward to reveal a hollow in the thick old wall behind it. Within the hollow, narrow stone stairs twisted to one side and rose out of sight.

I could feel my pulse racing, and I had to take a few deep breaths to steady myself. I was not at all sure that I wanted, after all, to climb those stairs into the unknown. I wedged the panel open with the screwdriver and fumbled new batteries into the failing torch, putting off the moment of decision. I could feel a slight down-draught on the stairwell, as if the unsealed door was sucking air from a ventilated place above. For some strange reason, its breath was sweet and slightly scented with lavender. At last, I forced myself to climb.

I knew that I had to be the first person to disturb the still, thick dust of that little chamber for many, many years. The room was small and low, its sides steeply pitched to follow the line of the roof, and snugly boarded to shut out all light and keep it secret. The floor under the dust was soft with the weave of a rug, while the light of my torch reflected back from the crowded surfaces of dark wood, tarnished brass, and silver and shadowed, painted faces.

Only in the center of the room could I stand upright, beside a high-backed, carved oak chair and a little table. Beyond them was the triangle of cobwebbed bricks that was the false wall that shut the room off from the rest of the hayloft. Along the wall stood a couch-like bed, spread with an embroidered coverlet and silken cushions. Most significant of all were the things on the table: a brass candlestick, and ink-well with a quill pen, a pile of age-blackened vellum sheets, a pewter plate and a mug, a leather jug and a little silver knife.

I was so stunned by what I had found that the torch wobbled in my hand as I gazed around me. Without a doubt, someone must have lived here once, sleeping and eating, sitting and writing in this secret chamber. And it could not have been from choice. The place was too small, dark, and claustrophobic to be bearable for too long. Whoever had lived here had lived in hiding, probably in fear. When I looked at the paintings, I knew who it had been.

Packed under the eves of the room was a jumble of what appeared to be hastily salvaged possessions, some of them blackened by smoke or singed by fire. Tarnished silver dishes were wrapped in brittle but still beautiful silk and velvet gowns. Leather bound books were heaped amidst crocks and pots, candlesticks, and goblets. Leaning against the wall were several portraits and a small painting of a girl on a horse. The faces in the portraits bore the unmistakable stamp of the Hyde-Grant family features. The girl on the horse was, of a certainty, the Melissa Anne Grant whose picture hung at the foot of the stairs in Pikersfield Manor House.

I picked up the painting and held it in the full light of my torch. It was quite small, no more than 18 inches square, an intimate study of the laughing girl in the blue velvet gown. Her hand rested affectionately on the dappled neck of her horse, and the long, blue, and gold embroidered panels of her saddle peeped from beneath the sweep of her skirts. Just as I had already seen a likeness of the girl, so I had already seen her saddle: it was down below in the hidden tack room.

Had I not been awkward in the darkness, holding both picture and torch, I might have missed the most important clue. I nearly dropped the painting and, as it turned in my hands, I saw that something was written on its back. The words were formed in a looping, extravagant script and, at first, I could make no sense of them. It was not until I tried saying each word aloud that I realized that every *f* should really be an *s*, and the meaning emerged.

"My horse Tapestry that I love most dearly for he is fleet, brave, and clever, a very paragon amongst horses."

78

This was written at the top of the back of the picture. Lower down and in a different colored ink, as if written later, were the words,

"I pray for my beloved brother Thomas, that Tapestry may bear him safe away from danger, but I sorrow to part from my dear and faithful horse. God grant the swift return of them both. I wait and weep for my loss."

Was this the explanation for which I had been searching? I sat in the high-backed, carved oak chair and gazed at the face of Melissa Anne Grant. Was she the Wailing Woman of Pikersfield? Had her brother and her horse never returned to her, so that she was waiting and weeping still, more than three hundred years later? If so, it was a dreadful torture for a spirit to bear. No wonder her sobs had the power to drown in misery anyone who heard them.

I glanced again around the room, but I could see nothing to prove either that I was right or I was wrong. I spread the scraps of parchment across the table, peering at each in turn. The sheets showed traces of writing, but they were dark and brittle, the looping script faded and mostly blotted out by time. The words on the back of the picture were the only evidence, as far as I could see, concerning the fate of Melissa Anne Grant.

I recalled what Mr. Hyde-Grant had told me, the first time I met him, about the Jacobean mansion that had been her home until Cromwell's troops burnt it to the ground. The girl disappeared and was never heard of again. She had never lived, he had said, at the Manor House, but he was wrong. From the evidence all around me, I was sure that she had escaped from the Roundheads and hidden here with what few of her family treasures she could save.

There was one thing wrong with my theory – how had Melissa Anne found the time and the help to make such a cunning hiding place in the sudden emergency? Melissa Hyde-Grant had already given me the answer to that. The hiding place was already in existence, long before Cromwell struck at Pikersfield. I had discovered the priest's hole for which Mr. Hyde-Grant had searched Pikersfield Manor in vain. This little chamber must have been the secret place in which the persecuted Roman Catholics of the time hid their fugitive priests.

I realized, also, that I was not the first person to find this room, since the tragedy of Melissa Anne Grant came to its mysterious conclusion and her hiding place was lost to human knowledge. Melissa Hyde-Grant's great, great grandfather must have been here before me. He was the Old Master of Mr. Poppy's enigmatic ramblings.

The Old Master must have come to the conclusion that nothing could be done to lay the ghost, who was condemned to wait and weep for all eternity. With the help of Mr. Poppy's grandfather, he had sealed up the old tack room to make sure that she should never again be disturbed. But he could not resist keeping just the one reminder of her. He had taken the Van Dyke portrait of her from this room and hung it at the foot of the stairs, to leave later generations to puzzle over where and when it had been found in the Manor House, and how it came to be there.

I felt drained of emotion, but my curiosity was only partially satisfied. There seemed to be nothing left to find, and nothing I could do about the unhappy ghost. Both the old master and Mr. Poppy had reached the same conclusion, and I was forced to agree with them: Melissa Anne Grant must remain locked away with her secrets and her sorrow.

I took one last, lingering look around the little chamber, replaced everything as I had found it, and turned to go.

Only then did I notice the hole in the wall at the top of the stairs. An area of stone work, level with the floor, had been removed and, when I crouched down and shined my torch into the cavity, I could see that it reached back a long way. It went not only through the depth of the stable block wall, but also through the thickness of another ancient wall beyond. The wall beyond could be only that of the Manor House, because the oldest wing of the stable block stood tight against the back of the oldest part of the house.

The hole was just wide and high enough for a fully grown man to crawl into it on his stomach. I lay flat on the floor and pushed my head and shoulders into the cavity, holding the torch close to my face. The other end was blocked by a rough wooden surface. I tested it with my fingertips, but the wood did not yield to my touch.

I lay there, my nose almost touching the square of timber, and tried to work out, from the geography of the Manor House, just where the short tunnel would emerge. And then it came to me. The dimly lit landing at the head of the back stairs from the kitchen passageway, the paneled wall with no doors or windows in it, the place where I had had the strange experience of seeing, hearing, and smelling things that were not there. My face was pressed against the reverse side of the wall paneling, inches from the landing floor.

There was bound to be some clever contrivance – a spring, a catch, or a simple pivot, as with the secret panel below – that would open the small bolt-hole to allow a hunted priest to escape from the house into this hiding place, but I did not want to find it. I had already made up my mind that Melissa Anne's secret must be kept. To open up yet another entrance to her lost room would be pointless. I wriggled backwards until I was clear of the tunnel, went down the stairs, and carefully closed the panel behind me.

I knew I ought to tell Mr. Hyde-Grant what I had discovered. There were many valuable things hidden in the little chamber and, by right, they belonged to him. More important than that, Mr. Hyde-Grant was, undeniably, the blood, family, and kin of which Mr. Poppy had spoken as being the only means by which Melissa Anne's unrest could be brought to an end.

He was also a cold, hard, thoroughly unpleasant man who had called the Wailing Woman a silly legend. He would never believe she existed, yet alone care enough to find a way to end her tears. But he would be greedy enough for her antique possessions, and I was reluctant to give him the satisfaction of getting his hands on them. It was not as if I was stealing his family heirlooms. They remained where they had always been, he just hadn't found them yet. I couldn't help but muster a wry smile at the thought, as I lugged the steps back through the stable buildings.

Chapter Nine

Melissa was an extremely difficult patient and her legs appeared to be paralyzed. She lay in bed, refusing even to be lifted into a chair or carried out of her room, and she demanded constant attention. She spent her first day home from hospital crying for her father, and when he failed to return she became emotionally unpredictable. Her moods swung from pitiful tears, when she clung to my mother for comfort, to fits of unreasoning temper, when she could not bear to have anyone near her and demanded to be left alone.

My mother was worn out by worry and lack of sleep. Mrs. Poppy worked extra hours, but was very grumpy about it. She maintained that Melissa had a mental problem and needed to see a specialist, but she didn't put it even that politely. I helped as much as I could, even though Melissa's dislike of me remained as strong as ever and she could hardly bear to have me in the room. So much for gratitude, I thought, after I had gone to so much trouble to arrange that wretched riding lesson! Mom needed to have at least a few hours sleep each night, so Melissa had to put up with me whether she liked it or not. After a couple of days an uneasy truce developed between us, then everything was made even more difficult because Mrs. Poppy walked out.

There was no doubt that Mrs. Poppy had seen the ghost. The night after I discovered the priest's hole, Mrs. Poppy was late leaving work and it was already dark when she went out to the yard to feed the cats. Minutes later, she staggered back into the kitchen white-faced and shaking, almost incoherent with terror. Mom had to administer several swallows of cooking sherry before the trembling woman was able to gasp out her story.

"Dreadful it was, all white and floaty, floating about inside them stable windows," she moaned. "I saw it with these very eyes, I did, gliding along in the moonlight with no head! 'Tisn't right, Mrs. Hurst, 'tisn't Christian and I'm off. Sorry to leave you in the lurch when you needs the help, but 'tisn't Christian and I can't be doing with it." She tore her aprons from the hook behind the door, packed her comfortable working slippers into her bag and was gone.

The whole thing sounded highly improbable to me, but still I was worried. By now I knew more than anyone living about the Wailing Woman of Pikersfield, and a floating, headless, white figure did not fit into the story at all. But down-to-earth, cynical Mrs. Poppy was not the sort of person to give way to over-imaginative hysterics. Had my meddling with the hidden room stirred up something else altogether?

Then the village became restive with rumors that the Wailing Woman had returned. The shepherd checking his flock one night in the field behind the orchard saw a white figure floating out of the stable yard and hovering under the apple trees. He immediately reported the matter to everyone in the bar of the Clarendon Arms, drowning his terror in alcohol until the ghost had acquired a trail of spectral vapor and an unearthly, wailing voice.

The next night, a woman walking her dog glimpsed a

pale form drifting behind the gates of the Manor House. She fled screaming through the estate, and roused half the neighborhood. In the morning, she and Mrs. Poppy held court in the village shop, comparing notes and making ghoulish conjectures in front of a crowd of open-mouthed housewives. Pikersfield became gripped by ghost mania, so the haunting was an established fact and I had to believe it.

Mrs. Poppy, the shepherd, and the dog-walking lady had all definitely seen something. As a result, Mom could find no one prepared to take Mrs. Poppy's job and my worry was rapidly turning to alarm. Had I released some dark, sinister force when I opened the secret panel and disturbed Melissa Anne's possessions? If so, what could I do about it? I would just have to lie in wait and try to see this ghost for myself.

Melissa had had a bad day. It was almost a week since the accident, and she had become more difficult with each day that passed. She had been fractious and querulous all morning, complaining bitterly of boredom, then pathetic and tearful all afternoon. By evening she had worked herself up into one of her "just go away and leave me alone" tempers. I was sitting with her while Mom caught up on some sleep, and I was only too happy to oblige.

"If I do leave you on your own for a while, you must promise not to ring our bell and wake Mom," I told her.

"I might."

"I won't go then."

"Alright, I promise, but you must not go too far away, so you can hear me if I call. Don't go outside and leave me alone, will you? You might get frightened by the ghost if you do." Melissa giggled. "I think it's really funny that the ghost has come back and is frightening everybody!"

"Oh, do you!" I said sourly. Trust Melissa to enjoy other people's troubles. I wished I hadn't told her about it.

"You won't leave the house, though, will you?"

"No, I won't." I crossed my fingers as I made the promise, because that was exactly what I intended to do. I hoped the ghost would see fit to put in an appearance, because I would not have long to watch for it.

I plumped up Melissa's pillows, put water glass, books, and television remote control within her reach, and left the room. I waited outside the door for a few minutes, to make sure that she kept her word and didn't ring her bell, then sprinted downstairs and out of the back door.

It was a lovely summer's night with a full moon riding high in a cloudless sky. I walked for a while in the orchard, breathing deeply to clear the taint of sickroom from my lungs, then made my way to the stable yard. I squatted in the garage doorway, beside the cats' empty bowls, and hoped that Muff and her kittens would come to keep me company, but there was no sign of them as I started my vigil.

I waited. Time passed. Nothing happened. I was not surprised. Ghosts don't usually turn up to order and, to be honest, I still didn't believe in this one. I was sure there had to be some other, more rational explanation for the village hysteria. I could not leave Melissa for much longer and my legs were getting cramped, so I stood up. Still there was nothing to see but moonlight glittering on the stable windows. Then a flicker of movement caught my eye. There it was! The pale figure was floating rapidly along inside the windows of the oldest wing of the stable block. It had passed the first window, vanished, reappeared at the second, and disappeared behind the doors, then appeared at the next window, reflecting flickers of moonlight from its billowing shroud as it sped. It was in the middle block now, directly opposite me, fluttering without a sound, just as Mrs. Poppy had described it. Now it was winging its way down the new stable block towards the garage door, and I could hear its dreadful sobbing.

My heart hammered my fear. The floating apparition had passed the last window and, any second now, I must meet it face to face. I was desperate to run but knew I must stay.

Sobbing with terror, and with my lace nightdress billowing about her, Melissa hurtled through the door and fell into my arms.

"I heard it. I heard the ghost. I heard her crying," Melissa gasped. She was starting to wheeze.

"Calm down. Breathe slowly and deeply." To my surprise Melissa did as she was told. She made an effort to control her panting so she could speak again.

"I heard the ghost sobbing. There's a door that I've never seen before, right at the end of the old wing, and I went in to look for the cats. She was crying and it was awful. You must believe me!"

"I do believe you. I've heard her myself."

"You have?" Melissa's eyes widened with this further shock. Despite the warmth of the night she was barefoot and wearing only a nightdress. She began to shiver violently, and her voice rose in a wail of hysterical wheezing and sobbing. At a sudden crash of noise behind us, Melissa started to scream. I spun round to see stirrup lights and reflective leg boots bobbing out of the darkness towards us, as two horses pounded up the drive.

"Anna, is that you?" Rich's voice called.

"Quick!" Ginny's voice interrupted, "We need your help." They were close enough now for me to see their worried faces. "The gray has ... "

"Not now, Ginny, can't you see I'm having a crisis!" I snapped. "Melissa, calm down for heaven's sake!" I shook Melissa by the shoulders, but she continued to scream.

"Want any help?" Ginny sounded more than willing.

"No, leave her to me. Melissa, be quiet!" I slapped her hard round the face, and the noise stopped as if someone had thrown a switch.

"Get her inside before she catches pneumonia," Rich said. He dismounted, took off his jacket and put it round Melissa's shivering shoulders. "What happened?"

"I thought she was paralyzed!" Ginny accused.

"If you want to know, you'll have to come in. Put the horses in the orchard."

I manhandled Melissa through the back door and into the kitchen, where I opened all the stove doors and sat her down in front of the blast of heat. She hugged Rich's coat around her and crouched in the chair like a frightened animal. I had just pushed the kettle onto the hob, to make her a hot drink, when Mom came into the kitchen through one door, Ginny and Rich through the other.

"I thought I heard hooves and screaming!" Mom was trying to gather her wits as she knuckled sleep from her eyes, then she registered the fact that Melissa was sitting in front of the stove, looking very much the worse for wear. "Oh Anna, what have you done to the poor child now?"

I bit back a sharp retort, but before I could think of anything sensible to say, Melissa whispered, "I heard the ghost crying in the stables. I went for a walk to look for the cats, and I heard the ghost. It wasn't Anna's fault. I made her leave me on my own, just as I always do when I want to go for a walk."

"I told you she was faking it!" Ginny said. "And now she's really flipped!"

88

"Shut up Sal, you'll only make things worse," Rich commanded. He was searching cupboards for mugs and cocoa.

Mom gathered Melissa in her arms and sat her on her lap, like a small child. "Now let's get this straight, dear. You say you went for a walk. How could you do that when your legs don't work?"

"There is nothing wrong with my legs, there never was." Melissa kept her head bent against Mom's shoulder, and wouldn't look any of us in the face. "I thought if I was really ill, really, really ill, my father would stay at home, but he didn't. Then I had to keep on pretending because I didn't know how to stop, and if everyone had found out they would hate me even more and go away too. Being ill and paralyzed is very boring. I had to go for walks, or I'd have gone mad. I wanted to see Muff and the kittens. I go to see them every night."

"But you are allergic to cats." Mom was puzzled. "Animal fur gives you a rash."

"No it doesn't. I pretended that too, with felt-tip to get Mrs. Poppy into trouble. I love cats. I love horses as well, that was why I tricked Anna into letting me ride Tess. If I'd asked you and my father, you'd have found out about all my pretends."

Mom looked up at me, anguish in her eyes. "Oh Anna, I'm so very, very sorry!"

It's alright Mom, at least you believed me," I croaked. Seeing Mom feeling such hurt was even worse than being hurt myself. She managed a weak smile and turned back to Melissa.

"You don't have to pretend anything more, Melissa," she said, gently. "Tell me everything, then you will feel better and we can make a fresh start."

We sat round the stove, sipping hot chocolate, while Melissa poured out her confessions in a cleansing flood. She had discovered, when she was quite young, that her parents paid attention to her if she had an asthmatic attack or trouble with her leg, but it was about the only time they did so. As far as I could gather, they had never wanted a family, and they were both far too involved with their work to have much time for their daughter. Melissa tried to gain their attention by pretending to be more ill than she was, but all that happened was that her mother left and her father employed a series of housekeepers, and then my mother, to take care of the problem for him.

Either consciously or subconsciously, Melissa had tried to drive the housekeepers away to force her father to come home. She had intended to do the same to Mom and me, but then discovered she couldn't bear to lose my mother. Unfortunately, she had become convinced that no one would ever like her or stay with her simply for herself, and the only way she knew to keep someone's attention was to use the same tricks and deceits she had practiced on her parents.

The tragedy of it all was that her pretended asthmatic attacks, because she got so overwrought, frequently turned into real ones. In the end, even Melissa could not tell where pretence ended and real illness began. Obvious to all of us was the underlying reason for Melissa's disturbed behavior – the continuing absence of her neglectful, unloving father.

"The ghost feels the same way that I do." Melissa at last sat up and looked me in the face. "She is miserable because she has lost someone she loves and is left alone. I could hear it in her voice."

It gave me a jolt that Melissa had so accurately divined the truth.

"Now, I thought we had agreed, Melissa, no more pretends," my mother said. "There are no such things as ghosts."

"Yes, there are. Honestly, I heard the ghost," Melissa insisted.

"She did," I said, reluctantly. "I've heard her too. She exists alright. The ghost everyone kept seeing was only Melissa wandering about in the dark in her nightdress, but there is a real one."

Ginny and Rich were gaping at me as if I'd grown a second head.

"Anna dear, don't be so foolish," Mom protested, then she raised her hand to silence my reply. "No, no more! I think I've had enough for one night. I must get Melissa to bed. We will talk about it in the morning."

When Mom and Melissa had left the kitchen, Ginny leaned back in her chair and let out a long breath. "Wow," she said, shaking her head. "I'm glad that's all over! I really can't handle heavy emotional scenes! Do you think Melissa is cured now?"

"You can't mend a broken leg overnight," Rich said. "I should think that broken emotions are much the same. Melissa is bound to need our help and understanding for quite some time. We'll just have to make allowances. Poor little kid! We've been thinking she's just a spoiled, unpleasant brat, and all the time she was living in a sort of personal hell!"

"I could kick myself for not realizing," I admitted. I felt wretchedly guilty for all the unkind thoughts I'd harbored about Melissa. I of all people should have realized what she had been going through. I made the mental resolution that from now on I would do everything in my power to make it up to her.

"Anyway," I changed the subject, "why were you two galloping about in the countryside in the dark?"

"Oh heck!" Rich exclaimed. "I must phone my parents, they'll be worrying. All this Melissa business made me clean forget about the gray."

"He's gone," Ginny said. "Vanished without trace."

Chapter Ten

"Vanished without trace" was a Ginny exaggeration, but the end result was the same: the gray had gone. The horse-watch scheme had run smoothly for a couple of days, until that afternoon when Charlie Trent had taken a turn on duty. When Rich arrived, driven in his father's car to relieve him, Charlie, who was not a horse enthusiast anyway, was engrossed in *Wisden* magazine in the hide across the lane, and the gray's field was empty.

The paddock gate was standing open, but it was unlikely that the gray, in search of better grazing, had pushed it open on his own and strayed away. The gate was heavy on its broken hinges and needed a hefty shove to shift it at all. But, just in case that was what had happened, mounted search parties were quickly organized. While the riders scoured the countryside, Rich's father drove the road to Pikersfield, asking at houses and farms if anyone had seen a tall, dapple-gray horse either alone or being led.

By nightfall, the searchers had a pretty good idea of what had happened. A jogger had seen a fat man leading a gray horse, not far from the gray's field and going in the Pikersfield direction. Inquiries at the local garage and the Clarendon Arms revealed further sightings of a stout man leading a dapple-gray horse towards the new Pikersfield estate. A woman who lived on the edge of the estate said she had heard hoof-beats passing her gate at dusk.

Ginny and Rich had ridden round the estate in the dark, hoping that, if the gray was there somewhere, he would hear Pearly and Mr. Big and call to them. They had no success.

"I never for a minute thought that we would," Ginny said. "I mean, how can you hide a thumping great horse like the gray on a housing estate, unless you stuff him into someone's living room?"

"Not on, is it?" Rich agreed. "The fat man was probably taking a short cut through the estate to the main Chawton road. I bet he's long gone now, and the gray with him."

"What about people at the other end of the estate, did anyone there see him?" I asked.

Ginny shook her head. "No, not that there were many people around to ask by then. They were all glued to the telly or gone to bed."

"Garages," I suggested. "He might be in a garage. Mr. Sams said that his owner used to live on the estate and has friends there."

"Stupid idea," Ginny said. "What would be the point? You can't hide a horse in a garage for very long without people finding out. The bottom line is that the owner doesn't want the ASPCA to know who he is, so he's got to vanish himself and his horse as fast as possible. Rich is right. He got well away from the district tonight, and we'll never see him or the gray again."

We had talked long into the night and, by then, it was far too late for Rich and Ginny to make the long ride back across the moors to Swallowbridge. They decided to leave Pearly and Mr. Big to munch their way round the orchard, while they camped in armchairs. I was very upset by the loss of the gray and argued that we should keep searching tomorrow but, in the end, I had to admit that what they said made sense. My dream horse was gone for good.

"What's all this nonsense about ghosts, Anna?" Ginny asked, when I brought them down pillows and blankets. "You were only humoring Melissa, weren't you?"

Like my mother, I had had quite enough for one night. "Tell you in the morning," I said, hoping they would forget all about it.

A very subdued Melissa joined us for breakfast, followed by Mom wearing smart clothes instead of her usual casual ones.

"Melissa has promised to be on her best behavior today," Mom said. "I must go to Oxford, but I know she will be perfectly alright with you to look after her, Anna."

My mother and I had been too close for too long to need mere words to make peace between us. It was thanks to my mother that I had not fallen apart, as Melissa had done, when my father left, and I had been very selfish to resent sharing my mother's generous heart with Melissa, who needed her care far more than I had done. My mother had been right all along. She had said from the very start that Melissa's odd behavior was a cry for help, and I should have listened to her. Mom and I smiled at each other, silently acknowledging faults on both sides that were best forgiven and forgotten.

"I am going to see Mr. Hyde-Grant," Mom said, with an ominous edge to her voice. "I have a few home truths to tell him, and they are best said face to face! Now Melissa, wasn't there something you were going to say to every-one?"

"Sorry about the accident. It was all my fault. I should have done as you told me." Melissa's head was lowered and her face was flaming.

"Good enough," Rich grinned. Ginny grunted non-committally.

Melissa spooned cereal in silence until we heard Mom's car crunch away down the drive, then she turned urgently to me.

"Anna, you must tell me what you know about the ghost! I was awake all night thinking about her. When did you hear her? What was it like?"

"Give it a rest. I thought you had reformed," Ginny snapped.

I had determined never to tell anyone about the secret chamber, but now I felt I owed it to Melissa to prove that, for once, she was not behaving irrationally. As far as the Wailing Woman was concerned, if Melissa was out of her mind, so was I. I told them the whole story.

"You dark horse, you!" Rich exclaimed. "I can't believe you kept something like this all to yourself! First hearing a ghost, then going off on your own and finding that room, and you never said a word to anybody!"

"What else could I do?" I protested. "If I'm right and the sobbing voice is the earth-bound spirit of Melissa Anne Grant waiting for her horse and her brother to come back, then there's nothing anyone can do about it. They have all been dead and dust for centuries. No one is ever going to come back. The place is best shut up and left alone."

"I just don't believe I'm hearing this!" Ginny jeered. "I can't believe it's you, Anna Hurst, sitting there so seriously and talking such crap. The nearest thing to a ghost there has ever been round here is Melissa in a nightdress."

"If Anna says she heard something, I believe her," Rich said.

"Oh c'mon!" Ginny was not to be convinced. "The wind in the roof was all she heard."

"I heard it too," Melissa insisted. "It wasn't the wind, I know. Anna, I want to see the room, please. I must feel what it is like. I must feel if she is still there."

Ginny snorted her scornful disbelief, and began to crash the breakfast dishes into the sink.

"Alright," I agreed, but with a dragging reluctance. I did not want to go back there, but I had to do so for Melissa's sake. "We'd better hunt up some torches, it's pitch dark up there. You don't have to come if you don't want to, Ginny."

"Just try to stop me! You've all gone crazy, and you need someone sane to keep an eye on you!"

Funnily enough, it was Ginny who drew back as I opened the door to the hidden tack room.

"Don't worry, we won't hear anything in here during daylight. The legend says the ghost cries only at night." I gave her a triumphant grin.

"It's not that at all," Ginny bristled. "I don't like dark, dirty places and I hate spiders!" She forgot all about spiders when I uncovered the sidesaddle. She wanted to lift it down from the rack to see how it was stuffed and how the girth straps worked. Rich stopped her.

"I don't think we ought to touch it, we might damage it," he warned. "Does it matter how it's put together? It's just very old and incredibly beautiful. It should be in a museum."

"Never!" Melissa laid her hand on the worn, blue velvet seat. "It belongs here, it belongs to Melissa Anne."

"That's nonsense. She's dead," Ginny told her sharply.

The panel pivoted open, and we climbed the stairs.

97

Obviously, my description had not been enough to prepare them for the shock of actually seeing the cramped chamber and all it contained. Even I, who had been there before, was dumbstruck by the tragic atmosphere of the lonely hiding place, and the pathetic evidence of those few salvaged possessions. Our torches lit the room, and it was several minutes before anyone spoke.

"She must have sat in this chair." Melissa broke our silence. She took the two paces from the stair head to the oak chair, and ran her hands over its carved back.

"Now you are being melodramatic!" Ginny scoffed. She was flashing her torch at the ceiling. "There, what did I tell you? Ventilation holes!" A row of holes had been drilled in the planks, high in the apex of the boarded roof. "I bet the wind fairly howls through them. There's your Wailing Woman for you."

Melissa ignored Ginny. She picked up the little painting of the girl on the horse, and sat in the carved chair, as I had done, staring at it.

"You're right, Anna," she said. Ginny and Rich bent over her shoulder, to shine their torches full on the picture. "It is Melissa Anne Grant alright, the girl in the portrait on the stairs. She was here. She sat in this chair, ate from this dish, and slept on that bed. I'm sure she is still here. I can sense it."

"You don't have any sense," Ginny muttered.

"She looks so happy in her portrait, and in this picture. I wonder what happened to make her so miserable?" Melissa turned the painting over. "I can't make out what it says, Anna, can you read it for me, please?

"My horse Tapestry," I read, "that I love most dearly for he is fleet, brave, and clever, a very paragon amongst horses. I pray for my beloved brother Thomas that Tapestry may bear him safe away from danger, but I sorrow to part from my dear and faithful horse. God grant the swift return of them both. I wait and weep for my loss."

"It all sounds pretty obvious to me," Rich said.

"Yes, but there must be so much more to the story than that," Melissa protested. "Why was she hiding here on her own? What was the danger her brother ran away from, and why did he leave her behind? Obviously he never came back, so why not, and what happened to Melissa Anne in the end? I have to know. I'll go mad if I don't find out!"

Ginny opened her mouth, obviously about to say something else scathing, but Rich silenced her with a look that would have withered a lesser mortal.

"There might be something else in the room that will give us a clue," I said, "but if there is, I couldn't spot it last time."

I did not like the feeling of intruding into something personal and private, as Rich and I sorted carefully through the items stacked under the eves. I feared, too, that we might damage the fragile fabrics and valuable old books. Rich's comment, that the saddle should be in a museum, had made me realize that all these things ought to be rescued and preserved by someone who knew what they were doing. Mr. Hyde-Grant would have to be told.

"Hey, look what I've found!" Ginny had pulled the coverlet from the bed to reveal a small trunk that had been draped and hidden at its foot. The trunk was of leather studded with brass nails, and had a rounded top. "Give me a hand to get it open, Rich, I don't think it's locked, just stuck."

Ginny held the torch close to Rich's prying fingers, as he pushed a coin between lid and catch, levering it up and down. With a snap and a brief hiss of in-rushing air, the lid opened. The room was filled with the sweet scent of lavender, as fresh as the day it had been picked who knows how long ago. The torchlight glittered on something gorgeous inside.

"Please, I must do this!" Melissa said. Instinctively, we all shuffled out of the way as she knelt on the floor and, with great reverence, began to unpack the trunk. The glitter was coming from a gold crucifix that lay, with a string of pearl and ivory rosary beads, on the top.

"This is more proof that it was Melissa Anne," Melissa said, "because she was a Roman Catholic. The Grants were all Roman Catholics and supporters of the King. My father is forever rambling on about the English Civil War. It's boring so I ignore most of it, but I remember about the Grants. Anna must be right about this room being the priest's hole, especially as it has that little tunnel into the house."

Beneath the cross, wrapped in silk layered with dried sprigs of the lavender that now strongly perfumed the room, were the more personal possessions of a wealthy, fashionable young lady of the Stuart era. Some were very fine and costly, others were touching in their simplicity. Melissa lifted out a pair of gauntlet gloves of kid leather with a flowing design of birds and flowers embroidered on the cuffs. They were made for the slender hands of a woman, and were still soft and supple.

"This trunk must have been air-tight, to preserve everything in this condition. I do hope taking them out won't ruin them," Melissa worried.

"How else are we expected to look at them? It was bound to get opened some time," Ginny argued. "Anyway, these won't spoil! Boy oh boy, did Melissa Anne love pearls!" Ginny held a string of pearls that glowed with creamy luster in the torchlight. There were earrings and bracelets to match. Melissa did not seem to care for the valuable jewels. She was more interested in a plain gold locket that contained a miniature of a serious-faced young man and a curl of pale hair.

"Do you think this was Melissa Anne's brother Thomas?" she asked.

"Has to be," Rich agreed. "He has the same blue eyes and they could almost be twins, apart from the fact he looks a bit glum."

The trunk was nearly empty. As well as the gloves and jewelry, we had found lace collars, ribbons, lawn handker-chiefs, even a pair of silk stockings, but none of these things told us more than we already knew about Melissa Anne Grant. All that was left, at the bottom of the box, was a bundle of thick, folded squares of paper tied together with satin ribbon. Melissa teased one open, but the parch-ment began to crack in her hands. There were brown stains running along the folds, and the writing on it had faded un-til it was practically illegible.

"I can make out a date, I think, but nothing else." Melissa was about to re-tie the paper into its bundle.

"Hang on a minute!" Rich stopped her, his voice rising with excitement. "It looks like a letter to me! That broken blob was sealing wax that once held it folded shut and, see, at the top it says, 'The third day of November in the year of Our Lord 1642,' then something or other Melissa. The spelling is weird, though. And there, at the bottom, 'from the hand of your brother who loves you.' It's a letter to Melissa Anne from her brother, probably the Thomas who went away with her horse and left her."

Now we were all excited. With shaking fingers, Melissa unfolded more of the papers. The dates ranged from 1642 to 1645, but only here and there could we make any sense of the words. The handwriting was cramped, the spelling strange, and the ink had faded to be, in places, completely lost under the stains. Melissa began to cry with frustration.

"It's all here, I know it is, the whole story and we haven't a hope of reading it! But I've got to know. I must find out!"

"What about your father, Melissa?" I suggested. "He should be able to read the letters. Doesn't he do a lot of work with old documents?"

"Oh yes, he lives for stuff like this! He would go mad with excitement if he saw this." Melissa's tone was bitter as she gestured round the room. "But I can't ask him. I can't even talk to him any more."

"It looks like you'll have to try," Rich said, gently. "If knowing what is in the letters is so important to you, then you don't have any choice, though, to be honest, I can't see what difference finding out will make."

"You don't understand. You didn't hear the ghost crying," Melissa sobbed.

"This is an odd coincidence, Anna, or hadn't you noticed?" Ginny was again studying the painting of Melissa Anne and Tapestry. "This horse of hers is a dead ringer for our gray. It must be just as tall, the same striking dapple-gray color with black points, even the same pink snip on his nose. Manes and tails must have been worn much longer in those days! His mane is practically down to his knees, and laid on the wrong side, too. It looks like it could do with a good pulling session!"

"Oh I don't know," Rich laughed. "I think it makes him look very dashing. Good grief, you are right about him being identical to our gray. How strange!"

I was surprised that I hadn't spotted the similarity, but I could not see that it was of any importance. After all, dapple-gray is not an unusual color for a horse. But I was watching Melissa's face, and what I saw made me feel uneasy. A strange stillness had come over the girl, as she took in the fact that the gray horse, that we had tried to rescue but had lost, looked exactly like Melissa Anne's Tapestry. There was an odd, fey expression in her eyes and a far away tone to her voice when she spoke.

"Then the gray is bound to come back. He won't stay lost for long because fate intends him to be here with me. Don't you see? All this is meant to happen. Why else did Anna find this room, when no one else had found it for hundreds of years? There is another Melissa living in the house now – me! I look just like Melissa Anne, and I understand exactly how she feels. When the gray comes to Pikersfield Manor the circle will be complete, as fate intends it to be and, in the end, we will find out the reason why."

The certainty in Melissa's voice, plus the chain of coincidences that were all too exact to be mere chance, made my scalp prickle with apprehension. I remembered my disturbing conviction of being expected, the first time I saw the Manor House. I had experienced the frightening sensation of being dragged inevitably into something I did not understand. I had heard the ghost. I was being forced to accept the fact that something paranormal was taking place. Ginny, on the other hand, hadn't and wasn't.

"Except that fate has made a major blunder and mislaid Tapestry Mark Two! So much for your cranky theories, Melissa. You've just gone ghost crazy. Forget all about it, before the men in white coats come and take you away." Ginny, I could see, was thinking that Melissa had merely exchanged one kind of disturbed behavior for another. I was not sure.

103

That evening Melissa wrote to her father, asking him to come home. For the first time in her life she was able to give him a reason that, as she knew from unhappy experience, would lure him like a magnet far stronger than her own needs. Mr. Hyde-Grant would be unable to resist the news that the priest's hole of Pikersfield Manor had been found.

Chapter Eleven

With the gray gone, there did not seem to be much point in our working at the fruit farm any longer. Mr. Sams agreed with Ginny and Rich that the horse would be miles away by now, and there was nothing anybody could do to trace him. The owner was legally entitled to do whatever he liked with his own property, so our hands were tied. Mr. Sams told us that he knew of any number of deserving cases, if the horse rescue fund was burning a hole in our cash box, but we said no thank you, it wouldn't be the same.

Melissa continued stubbornly to insist that the gray was bound to come back into our lives, so we must keep the cash ready for when he turned up. In the cold light of day, away from the strange influence of the secret chamber, and in spite of the fact that the loss of the horse made me intensely miserable, the idea was too farfetched even for me to swallow. None of us believed that we would see the gray horse ever again but, because she was getting so much better and we did not want to upset her, we humored Melissa by not contradicting her.

As Rich had predicted, Melissa was not cured over night. She spent hours with my mother, talking through her problems and trying to come to terms with her feelings.

She had been so thoroughly spoiled in all the wrong ways for so long, that we still had uncomfortable moments when Ginny flared into a temper and Melissa sulked at not getting her own way. Nevertheless, Melissa was much easier to live with and, as a result, life was vastly more pleasant at Pikersfield Manor.

Mrs. Poppy came back to work after the Ghost of Melissa's Nightdress was explained to her. The news of the sham haunting spread rapidly through the village, by means of the village shop gossip club, and everyone managed to laugh at themselves for getting so worked up over it. In their minds at least, the Wailing Woman of Pikersfield was laid to rest.

Not so with Melissa. She remained totally obsessed by Melissa Anne Grant and the mystery of what had become of her. I could not bring myself to tell my mother about the real ghost. There would be time enough for that when Mr. Hyde-Grant came home – if he ever came.

Day after day passed with no word from him, while Melissa became increasingly distracted, fey, and moody with the strain of waiting. My mother noticed Melissa's moodiness and began, again, to worry about her, which, in turn, worried me. I had to find a way to take Melissa's mind off the ghost and keep her occupied, so I suggested to Mom that Rich and Ginny should stay at the Manor for a few days because the company would do Melissa good. Mom thought it an excellent idea, and they moved in the next day, bringing Pearly, Mr. Big, and Tess with them. I was determined that, when the time came for them to go home, Tess would not go with them.

Cleaning out the stables was a good way to keep Melissa busy. After a day of mops, buckets, brooms, and hard work, the newest wing of the stable block was ready for use. We

held an opening ceremony when Melissa smashed the pad-
lock with a hammer, the keys having been long since lost,
and swung wide the double outer doors. The horses were
pleased to come in from the orchard during the heat of the
day, to be away from the tormenting flies. The tack room
smelled once again of well-soaped leather, and the feed
store re-awakened to the clatter of buckets and bin lids.

Ginny insisted that, if Melissa was serious about learning to ride, she must learn all about stable management as
well, so she ought to do her share of the work. Poor
Melissa! After a session of mucking out the straw beds,
filling hay nets, or strapping the horses, she would be
wheezing and gasping into her inhaler. Although Melissa
had used her illness, by pretending that it was far worse
than it was to get attention, there was no doubt that her
asthma remained a problem she must live with.

Her leg, too, still bothered her, although to a decreasing
extent as the muscles strengthened. By the end of each day,
especially after a riding lesson, Melissa's limp was noticeably worse and looked painful. But now she never made a
fuss about it. To her surprise, she discovered that her un-
complaining determination to carry on regardless, earned
her far more sympathy and respect than her tantrums had
ever done, especially from Ginny. Ginny was a great ad-
mirer of guts, and she declared that the new Melissa was
one of the gutsiest people she had ever met.

Funnily enough Ginny became, out of the three of us,
Melissa's staunchest champion. Ginny tended to be an all
or nothing sort of person, inclined to see life in black and
white with no indeterminate shades of gray between. She
either liked people or hated them and, in hurting me,
Ginny's friend, Melissa had invited Ginny's uncompromising enmity. But now that Melissa had earned Ginny's sym-

pathy and respect, she had made herself an equally uncompromising friend.

Rich and I thought it odd when Melissa insisted that the stable spring clean be extended to the whole yard, especially the oldest wing of the block. Ginny backed up Melissa, so we didn't argue and spent another two days of hard, manual labor. Ginny got hold of a scrap merchant who removed most of the junk from the old wing, and we had a massive bonfire to get rid of the rest. Rich hammered the rough, old, wooden partitions back into place. The narrow stalls were primitive and the building, even with the outer door open, remained low and dark. It was not at all the kind of place that I would wish to stable a horse, but at least Melissa was satisfied, although she refused to say why.

Muff and her kittens were not so happy. They had been deprived of their mouse-hunting hideaway and were upset by all the noise and activity. They left in a huff and moved into the house. Very soon they were sleeping on our beds, begging for food at table, and tripping up Mrs. Poppy in front of the stove. My mother threw up her hands in horror, but Melissa wanted them to stay so the cats won the day. Muff looked very smug about their victory.

It was not long before Melissa asked to go for a ride, instead of riding boring circles in the orchard. The problem was that four of us wanted to ride, but we had only three horses. Rich found the solution when the scrap merchant's visit turned up an old bicycle, hidden under the junk. It was still sound, although horribly uncomfortable, and we fitted new tires and breaks to make it roadworthy. We rode every day, Melissa riding Tess and the rest of us taking turns on the bike.

A week had passed, and still we had heard nothing from Mr. Hyde-Grant. I was not surprised because Mom had returned from her visit to Oxford in a state of angry indignation: he was a selfish, unfeeling man, she said. He had shown no pleasure in hearing that Melissa was not as ill as we had supposed, no anger that she had deceived everybody, no sympathy for her mental distress, and no guilt over his neglect that had caused it. In fact, he had shown no emotion whatsoever, apart from relief that his problem was solved and Melissa would no longer have any excuse to interrupt his work.

In the end, Melissa gave up rushing to meet the postman every morning, hoping for a reply to her letter. I could have wept for her.

It was a very hot Friday morning. The horses needed new shoes, so Ginny, Rich, and I had ridden to the forge in Winterford in the early cool of the day, and by 10 a.m. we were on our way back to Pikersfield. We had just passed the gray's empty field when we were amazed to see Melissa, pedaling furiously towards us on our old crock of a bicycle. She managed to wheeze, "The gray...found him," before she dropped the bike in the road and collapsed onto the grass verge. Her face was pale and her chest heaved, as she took a deep pull at her inhaler.

"Steady, don't try to talk," I instructed. I flung myself from Tess' back and knelt beside Melissa. She was fighting her asthma and gasping with the urgency of what she wanted to say.

"Today market day Chawton. Saw advert in paper. Horse sale so watched estate from attic window. Garage, fat man, gray horse. Auctioneers' lorry, name on side. Horse looked awful. Get to Chawton. Buy him!"

"Of course we can't leave you," Ginny snapped.

"I'll stay," I said. "You two get going the shortest route,

Tess couldn't make the hedge. Phone Mr. Sams from the house."

After only a moment's hesitation, Ginny swung Pearly round in the lane and faced her at the hedge. Pearly jumped off her hocks from a standstill, cleared the obstacle and landed galloping. Mr. Big was hard on her heels, and they thundered away across the sheep field towards Pikersfield Manor. Tess churned circles beside me, jerking at her reins, and calling after her friends.

"Be quiet, you silly old mare," I soothed. "How are you feeling Melissa?"

"Fine," she lied. "Just give me a minute or two, and then I think I'll be able to ride Tess home, if that's okay with you."

I made her sit still for another 10 minutes, although I was as impatient as she was to get going. I was filled with admiration for Melissa. It had been very clever of her to keep her eyes open for anything that might bring the gray and his owner out of hiding. The rest of us had given up far too easily. A horse sale was the obvious chance for the fat man to off-load his problem horse without being out of pocket. It gave me no comfort to know that I had been right all along about the garage, and that the gray had spent all that time cooped up in such a prison. The fat man must be thinking that the hue and cry after him had died down by now, and he would be able to sell the horse and get away unnoticed. With luck, we would prove him wrong.

When Melissa's breathing had returned almost to normal, I legged her into Tess' saddle, retrieved the bike, and we made our slow way back to the Manor House. We were turning into the drive gates when the ASPCA van skidded to a halt in the road.

"Is the young lady alright?" Mr. Sams called. "Ginny is very worried about her."

"I'm better now," Melissa told him. "But why aren't you at the market, looking for the gray?"

"I dropped Rich and Ginny off there and came back for you. You are the only one of us who saw the fat guy. I might need you to pick him out in the crowd, if you feel up to it, that is."

"Of course I do," Melissa crossly insisted.

Chapter Twelve

Chawton Cattle Market was crowded, noisy, and stiflingly hot. All sorts and conditions of horses and ponies stamped, jostled and neighed, packed into the cattle pens or tied to the railings. Others were being trotted up and down the aisles to tempt buyers. An auctioneer selling tack in a shed shouted his patter above the bedlam, and crashed his gavel at regular intervals. A queue of restless animals fidgeted and kicked, waiting their turn to go into the auction hall ring. It was impossible to find Rich and Ginny in the milling throng. Mr. Sams elbowed his way through the crowd, while Melissa and I struggled to keep up with him.

The auction hall was a big building on the far side of the penning yard. Inside it, a semicircle of stone terraces rose round the sale ring. The steps were packed with people, some bidding, some examining their catalogues, and some idly watching and chatting. An elegant bay thoroughbred was being led around the ring by a white-coated auctioneer's assistant, while the auctioneer's voice rose above the hum of conversation to a higher and even higher asking price.

"There you are at last!" Ginny wriggled down the steps through the press of people. "The gray is not in the catalogue, or in any of the pens. I'm keeping an eye on the ring

112

while Rich keeps watch outside, but I'm sure our horse isn't here."

"Don't give up," Mr. Sams encouraged. "They sell the quality horses first. If the gray is in a poor state, his owner wouldn't bother putting him in the catalogue. He'll keep him out of sight, then push him in with the riff-raff at the end of the sale. I'll go and nose around the sheds. I know all the hiding places!" He grinned and was gone.

It became a long, weary wait for all of us in that stifling hall. Rich and Mr. Sams appeared at intervals with nothing to report, and Melissa went out with them several times, to see if she could spot the fat man or the lorry that had collected the gray, but neither were to be found. At last all the catalogued entries had been sold, and the late entries began to come into the ring. We kept a close watch on the door, hoping against hope that our gray might suddenly appear.

The crowd had thinned by now to leave, besides Ginny, Melissa, and myself, only a few grim-faced men in brown kennel coats.

"They are the slaughterhouse men," Ginny said. I tried not to watch as an old pony was sold for meat money. It seemed to me a wicked thing that, after a lifetime of faithful service, the pony should be sent alone and afraid to meet his end just because he was of no further use and his owner wanted to make a last few pounds out of him. I swore to myself that I would never sell Tess, even if it meant I could not ever have another horse, just in case such a thing happened to her. She had earned a comfortable old age and a peaceful end at home.

"Isn't it horrible," Melissa voiced my feelings. "I wish we were rich enough to fill all the stables at home with old ponies like that, and give them a happy retirement."

"Just the one will have to do for now, if he ever turns

up," I said. Melissa was not looking at all well. Ginny had dashed out to the burger stand in the yard to buy her a coke, and was sitting beside her on the step, making her sip it slowly between wheezes.

Then, running footsteps echoed through the hall and Rich sprinted up the terraces towards us. There was a sudden commotion in the yard beyond the doors of the sale ring. I could hear Mr. Sams' raised voice, people shouting and a flurry of movement. The brown-coated knackers men hurried outside, to see what was going on, just as our tall, gray horse stumbled into the ring.

"It's the fat man," Rich panted. "We saw him at the very last minute, and he's legging it with Mrs. Sams in hot pursuit. It's chaos out there, but I thought I'd better come in cause I've got the cash. You do the bidding, Ginny, you've got the loudest voice!"

But there was no one left to bid against. If there had been I don't think they, or even the knackers men, would have shown much interest in the thin, filthy animal that staggered in front of the auctioneer's rostrum. The tired auctioneer wanted to be done for the day, and he was selling without a reserve price. Within seconds, the gray was knocked down to Ginny for a fraction of our fruit picking money.

"I told you so," Melissa wheezed, "Tapestry is coming home."

"Just look at him! It's scandalous, it's wicked! He's in a far worse state now than when Anna first found him. And you let the fat man get away! How could you?" Ginny raved at poor Mr. Sams.

The gray swayed down the ramp of the ASPCA trailer and stood in the middle of the manor House stable yard, his head drooping almost to the cobbles. He must, indeed, have spent the last 10 days shut in a garage with no bedding and very little to eat. What weight he had gained, while we were looking after him, had melted away. His quarters and belly were crusted with dried dung, probably from having to lie in his own filth on a bare, concrete floor, his legs were cut, and he had a big hock.

"Win some, lose some," Mr. Sams said, philosophically. "We might get the fat guy yet. If he tries to collect his money from the market office, my colleague will nab him. What really counts is that the horse is safe. He is legally yours now, no one can argue with that." Mr. Sams was darting around the gray, taking pictures with a camera.

"Can't you leave him in peace?" Ginny complained.

"Evidence! Just a couple more," Mr. Sams grinned. "Knowing you and your friends he is not going to look like this for long!"

Ginny, mollified by the compliment, calmed down and handed the gray's rope to Melissa. "You might have some cranky ideas about why he's here, but here he is. You were right and you found him, so it's only fair you do the honors and take Tapestry into his stable."

"Tapestry, nice name. Is that what you are going to call him?" Mr. Sams asked.

"It doesn't look as if I have much choice," I said, dryly.

I was trying to be reasonable about the ownership of the gray. It was I who stumbled across him, starving in his bare paddock. It had been my idea to raise the money to rescue him. I was the one who needed a bigger mount but couldn't afford to buy a good one. I had grown to love him as if he were already my own. But, according to the bill of sale, Ginny, Rich, and I now owned him equally between us. It was fair, because they had worked just as hard to earn the

115

money. In reality they had picked a lot more fruit than I had done, but made no mention of the fact. Melissa, too, must have an interest. She had used her head to track the horse down, and I needed her stable and her land or else I could not afford to keep the gray. All the leftover earnings would be needed to pay the vet, who would have to treat the gray's legs. Nothing was turning out as I had planned and I hadn't even been allowed to choose the gray's name myself, but there wasn't a lot I could do about it.

Melissa led Tapestry through the double doors and along the walkway to his box, where Rich was putting the finishing touches to a deep straw bed. Pearly, Mr. Big, and Tess called from their stables and Tapestry, recognizing them, brightened up a bit and whickered back. He was even more interested in the warm mash I tipped into his manger. Melissa smoothed his sunken neck, and crooned to him while he ate.

"We'll have to watch his diet at first, or his system will go into overload and he'll scour," Ginny advised.

"I know, I know," I said, trying to hide my irritation. Ginny was inclined to think she knew better than anyone else and to take over.

"And," she went on, "you're not to disturb him by trying to clean him up tonight, or get the vet to look at his hock. That can all wait till tomorrow. Right now he needs peace and quiet."

"So why don't you shut up and give him some? We're not stupid, you know!" Rich told her, sharply.

"Er, I'd better get going now." Mr. Sams looked amused. "I think you'd better sort out who owns which bits of Tapestry before there are any more arguments!"

"What is going on here?" The angry voice boomed through the stables and made us all jump. I spun round to

116

see Mr. Hyde-Grant striding down the walkway towards us. He glared at Mr. Sams. "Who gave you permission to fill my stables with horses? If the trailer blocking my garage is yours, shift it, then shift these animals out of here."

"Daddy!" Melissa ran out of Tapestry's box, and her father gave a start of surprise. I don't suppose he had ever seen this Melissa before, radiating enthusiasm and joyful welcome. "I knew you'd come when you got my letter! Just wait until I tell you about the old stables."

"Stables! Is that all you've dragged me home to see? I thought it was something important." Mr. Hyde-Grant's face darkened with fury. He turned on his heel and delivered his parting shot over his shoulder. "I will have words with Mrs. Hurst about this. She will have to deal with you. I will not be staying."

The four of us bid a hasty good-bye to Mr. Sams, settled the horses, and hurried to the house. Mom, in a state of panic, was preparing a tea tray in the kitchen. Mr. Hyde-Grant, she said, was in his study and not at all pleased.

"That must be the understatement of the year," Ginny remarked.

"We've no choice," Rich said. "We'll have to beard him in his den. We can't let him go back to Oxford without even hearing Melissa out."

It quickly became apparent that although Melissa had longed for her father to come home, now that he was actually here she was totally terrified of him. She no longer had her shield of pretended illness to hide behind, so she retreated into trembling silence. With a sinking feeling, I realized that I would have to be the one to do the talking. I led the way and tapped on his study door.

"Come!" the voice rapped out, and we all trooped in.

"Yes?" He looked at me, impatiently.

"Er..." I cleared my throat nervously. "It was not about horses that Melissa wrote to you, Mr. Hyde-Grant, although it was about the oldest wing of the stables. There is a room hidden in the roof, and we think it is a priest's hole."

"Nonsense. I had a builder go over that roof after the gales last winter. He had to replace several tiles, but he said nothing about a hidden room underneath."

"He wouldn't have seen it from above. It's lined with boards and…"

"And it's just a hayloft. Priest's holes were usually cramped little hideaway-holes, not whole rooms."

"Tell him the entire story," Ginny interrupted. I did not want to do that. I had the feeling that if I made a mention of the Wailing Woman, Mr. Hyde-Grant would lose interest at once.

"Yes, tell me the whole story." He looked at his watch. "And make it snappy. I want to have something to eat and then get on my way."

So I launched into the story, starting from my finding the bricked-up tack room and making no mention of why I had been looking for it. Of course I had to get to the ghost eventually and, just as I had feared, his eyebrows shot up and he barked a skeptical laugh.

"The Wailing Woman of Pikersfield, you foolish girl, is just a story, a rural legend with its origins in a time when simple country folk were uneducated and superstitious. Of course I know about the room with the bricked-up window. My grandfather told my father all about it, and he told me. The old man claimed that, years before, he had locked away some accursed relic in there, but he was eccentric and senile – must have been nearly a hundred when he died!

118

There is nothing there, and it is most definitely not a priest's hole! Now, go away and leave me in peace."

"You are just not listening, are you?" Ginny shouted at him, losing her famous temper in a most spectacular manner. "There is a second hidden room upstairs. Call yourself a historian – you can't even be bothered to listen properly, yet alone go and investigate. Why don't you stop behaving like a bone-head and go and look at it!"

To my surprise, Mr. Hyde-Grant slapped his hand on his desk and roared with laughter. Perhaps he liked people who dared to stand up to him. He jumped to his feet and, with a mocking bow, opened the study door for Ginny. "Right, you red-headed little spit-fire, lead the way!"

By now, the yard was gray with dusk and the stable buildings were deeply shadowed. Our torches sliced through the gloom of the old wing. I heard Mr. Hyde-Grant gasp when the panel pivoted open in the wall, and I gave Melissa a push, so that it was she who led her father upstairs.

It had to be Melissa, I thought, who first took her father into Melissa Anne's last hiding place: it was only right. Ginny, Rich, and I hung back at the head of the stairs, not wanting to crowd the little chamber, and we held our torches aloft to flood the room with light. I had never seen a man so stunned. Mr. Hyde-Grant swayed and clutched at the newel post for support, his face turning quite white as he took it all in.

Melissa sat in the carved chair, watching her father's reactions. "Are you pleased?" she whispered.

"Pleased!" He stooped under the pitched roof, gently touching in turn the paintings and the books, the little table with all that stood on it, the couch and, finally, the picture of Melissa Anne and Tapestry. "Pleased? That is far too small a word. I can't think of any word huge enough to describe how I feel. But yes, Melissa, I am pleased."

"Turn the painting over and read what's on the back. It will explain why I need your help to find out the rest."

"You need my help to find out? I didn't think you were interested in such things but..." His voice trailed away as he studied the back of the canvas.

"Rich, get the trunk and open it. Show him the letters," Ginny called from behind us on the stairs. Rich wriggled past Mr. Hyde-Grant and pulled the trunk from the end of the bed. As lavender once more scented the room, Mr. Hyde-Grant dropped to his knees with a shout of excitement.

"The Henrietta Maria Crucifix, it has to be!" he exclaimed. He lifted the cross so that its jeweled face flashed in the light. "It was part of the dowry of Charles I's queen. There was quite a fuss when she gave it to a favorite lady-in-waiting. How extraordinary if that lady-in-waiting was Melissa Anne Grant. What a find!"

Mr. Hyde-Grant slowly unpacked the trunk, his face working with emotion. He would have lingered to examine each thing in turn but Melissa, kneeling beside him, took out the letters and thrust them into his hands.

"We think they are letters to Melissa Anne from her brother, but we can't read them," she said, with a quaver in her voice. "You will be able to read them. You have to read them, because I must know why she was here and what happened to her."

"Does it mean that much to you, Melissa?" he asked, with a gentleness I had thought him incapable of expressing. He gathered up the letters and put them on the table, then sat in the carved chair and looked round at us.

"I owe you all an apology, especially Melissa. What you

120

have found is of great historical importance. Some of these things are valuable, too, but that does not matter so much to me. It is their age and what they can tell us about a time long gone, a very important time in history that means so much more to me. I am delighted to discover that Melissa feels the same way that I do. Above all, I shall be forever in your debt, Anna, because it was your intelligent searching that found this room."

I colored with embarrassment, but I had to make him see that Melissa's peace of mind was more important than mere history. Mr. Hyde-Grant had got hold of the wrong end of the stick about Melissa's interest in the room, and Melissa seemed still too nervous to speak for herself.

"The point is, Mr. Hyde-Grant, can you read those letters?" I asked. "As you said, it means a lot to Melissa to find out about the ghost."

"Yes, given time and my lab equipment, I'll be able to decipher them quite easily." He picked up one of the discolored vellum sheets from the table. "And I think these, too, will bear looking at. Unless I'm very much mistaken, the hand that wrote these also wrote the words on the back of the picture."

"You mean, Melissa Anne wrote this?" Melissa took the paper from her father and smoothed it between her fingers.

"Yes, it may even be a rough sort of diary. But as for the ghost – no, I can't accept that. I think you have been letting your imaginations run away with you! Everything in this room must be listed, examined, and taken to a place where it can be safely preserved. I'm afraid the letters will have to wait until that is done. I'll get around to them one day."

Melissa's face was stricken. I, too, was upset. I had expected him to be able to read the letters to us more or less right away and put Melissa out of her misery. Mr. Hyde-

Grant was re-packing the trunk. Rich glanced over his head at me, and shrugged his resignation.

The sobbing began as a faint, hardly audible echo.

I saw from her expression that Melissa heard it too, although the others didn't seem to be aware of the sound. Then Rich glanced round uneasily, and Ginny lifted her torch to peer suspiciously at the ventilation holes in the roof. Mr. Hyde-Grant stiffened suddenly, standing in the center of the room and turning his head from side to side, as if he could not believe his ears. The sobbing gradually increased in intensity.

The crying voice became louder and louder until it filled the room. Now there could be no mistake. It came from everywhere at once, seeping from the walls, the floor, the furniture, the very air, until all rippled, and vibrated with the desolate voice of a misery that had so saturated the place that time alone would never blot it out.

Mr. Hyde-Grant, his face ashen, put his arm round Melissa and drew her tightly to his side. With his other hand he beckoned us closer. We huddled together in the center of the little secret chamber, and drowned in the awful weeping.

I could hardly bear the misery of it. Rich was biting his lip until it bled. Ginny had her hands clamped over her ears. Tears were streaming down the faces of Melissa and her father. Just when I thought I could not endure it for another second, the crying ended on a tremulous sigh. Light footsteps passed close beside us, tapped down the stairs, and faded into silence.

"Now I understand," Mr. Hyde-Grant said. "Now I truly understand!"

Chapter Thirteen

My mother was taken by surprise when we crowded through the back door, and Mr. Hyde-Grant declared that he was starving and why didn't we all eat together in the kitchen? She rose to the occasion, though, and was soon trimming chops while we pitched in to help with the vegetables. Melissa sat close to her father at the kitchen table, her face shining with happiness.

"So I was wrong," Ginny admitted. "There wasn't a breath of wind tonight, so it couldn't have been the holes in the roof. But you would think that my very first ghost would have had the decency to show herself! Didn't any of you see anything?" Ginny was trying to sound like her usual chirpy self, but I could see that she was severely shaken.

"I'm glad I didn't!" Rich shuddered over the potato peelings. "Just hearing her was bad enough."

"It has at least taught me a valuable lesson," Mr. Hyde-Grant said, seriously. "Shakespeare was right when he said that there are more things in heaven and earth then are dreamed of in our philosophy. I was guilty of having a closed mind, and that is an unforgivable fault in a researcher! In fact, today has taught me several lessons, some of them extremely painful ones."

Mom shot me an inquiring glance, and I realized that she

hadn't a clue what we were talking about. She might just believe it from the lips of Mr. Hyde-Grant, so I asked him to tell her. He duly recounted the whole story.

"Oh dear me, well I never!" Mom subsided into a chair, limp from the shock of it all. "But don't breathe a word about ghosts to Mrs. Poppy, or she will hang up her dusters for good. It's just one crisis after another in this house!"

"I trust you will find that the worst is over now," Mr. Hyde-Grant told her. He took Melissa's hand and held it in both his own. "I have been a very stupid man, Mrs. Hurst, so stupidly selfish and proud that I didn't even listen to you when you told me I had all the wrong priorities in life. As I said, I have learned my lesson. From now on, family comes first, and I realize that Pikersfield Manor can have no worth whatsoever unless it is, before anything else, a happy family home.

Mom began to sniff and look weepy. She had to busy herself again with the chops to hide her emotions. I was silent, absorbed by my own thoughts.

The ghost of Melissa Anne Grant might be condemned to an eternity of sorrowful unrest, but she had most certainly brought about a miracle at the Manor House. The shock of hearing her, the first time, had jolted Melissa out of her self-absorbed miseries, triggered her confession, and set her on the road to recovery. The ghost's sobbing tonight had brought Mr. Hyde-Grant to his senses, forcing him to take notice of his daughter and to reassess his whole life. It was, I thought to myself, a terrible tragedy that we could do nothing in return for Melissa Anne.

"How long will it take you to read the letters?" Melissa asked. Mr. Hyde-Grant had brought them down from the secret chamber, and they were packed safely in a box in his study.

"I'm not sure. Quite a few days, and I'll have to take them back to Oxford. No, don't worry," Mr. Hyde-Grant hastened to reassure Melissa, "I'll come home again, I promise."

"But can't you work on them here?"

"Not very easily. I will need the lighting and magnifying equipment I have at the university. Don't forget, I'm used to dealing with damaged old documents, and they must be correctly treated and preserved, or else they'll just fall to bits."

Our kitchen supper turned into quite a party. Mom and Mr. Hyde-Grant shared a bottle of wine that brought the roses to Mom's cheeks and smoothed away the tensions from before. Mr. Hyde-Grant kept us all laughing with his stories about eccentric professors and undergraduate howlers. I could understand why he had preferred Oxford to a home disrupted by Melissa at her worst, but it did not make him any the less to blame.

After supper Melissa insisted that her father come with us to check the horses and to hang the late night hay nets. It would not be a good idea, yet, to turn Tapestry out into the orchard with the others, so we were keeping them all in tonight, to be company for him in a strange place. Tapestry was lying down in his thick straw bed, too weary even to get up when I switched on the light.

"Isn't he handsome!" Melissa said. She knelt at his shoulder and gently rubbed his neck. Tapestry made a low, whickering noise deep in his throat, by way of greeting.

"He might be, given time." Mr. Hyde-Grant was leaning on the box door. "I don't know much about horses, but isn't he a trifle thin? I'd better tell shepherd he will have to find somewhere else for his sheep. That bag of bones is going to need every blade of grass he can get!"

125

It turned out that Mr. Hyde-Grant was pleased, after all, to see his stables back in use, especially as Melissa was so excited and enthusiastic about the horses. He listened, with a thoughtful expression, to the story of Tapestry's rescue, and to Ginny's glowing account of how well Melissa was learning to ride. It was then that a disturbing idea occurred to me. It was more than likely that Mr. Hyde-Grant had not yet gotten over his habit of bribing Melissa by buying her anything she wanted. If she had decided that she wanted Tapestry, I might as well kiss him good-bye right now. It was not a happy thought.

But at least I could take comfort from the fact that Tess' problems were now all over. Mr. Hyde-Grant said that of course she must stay at Pikersfield Manor, and, he promised her, whatever else happened, a stable for life. He invited Ginny and Rich, too, to stay for as long as they liked.

Early the next morning, Mr. Hyde-Grant left for Oxford, taking the box of letters with him.

I had not thought that Ginny and Rich would accept Mr. Hyde-Grant's invitation to stay for much longer at the Manor. We had already missed Pony Club camp – not that it hadn't been worth it for the sake of rescuing Tapestry – and now we were missing the summer horse shows and gymkhanas. Ginny was a keen competitor and Pearly was well-known in the area for her double clear rounds in show-jumping competitions, and for her speed in the jump-off that usually won her the class. Rich had not owned Mr. Big for very long, and would surely want to find out what he could do. I was surprised when they said they would stay, at least until Mr. Hyde-Grant returned.

Melissa, her obsession with Melissa Anne put on hold

for the while, was now obsessed with Tapestry. She spent hours with him in his box, grooming him until his dapple-gray coat shone, or just talking to him and feeding him tit-bits. I did not approve of the tit-bits, but Tapestry lapped up all the fuss and attention. He now called to Melissa whenever he saw her, whereas it had always been to me that he came first, at the gate of the sour little paddock of unpleasant memory. One morning, I tried to take over Tapestry's feeding, grooming and mucking-out myself, but Ginny took Melissa's side. After all, Ginny pointed out, we owed Melissa a debt for providing free board and lodging for our horse.

Since the night in the secret chamber, when we all heard the sobbing voice, Ginny had become even more protective of Melissa. They often went off on their own, and were forever getting their heads together for secret conferences. Quite by accident, one day, I could not help overhearing Melissa on the telephone. Ginny was standing beside Melissa, prompting her, and Melissa, obviously, was speaking to her father. I distinctly heard her say, "When you buy Tapestry."

My suspicions were confirmed when I broached the subject to Rich. We were riding together across the moors. Ginny and Melissa had stayed at home, occupied with some mysterious business of their own.

"Rich," I began, not sure how to put it without offending him. "Rich, would you ever sell your share of Tapestry to someone else?"

"Why? Do you want to buy us out? I guessed you would."

"You know I haven't got a penny to my name! The vet's and farrier's bills have used up all the rest of the rescue fund, and that was partly yours anyway. I want to pay you back eventually, but I can't afford it at the moment. No, I mean sell him to someone else, before I have the chance to save up to buy him from you myself."

"It depends on who it is, and why they want him."

"If someone offered you a lot of money – and let's face it, he will be worth a lot of money when he is fit – someone who could afford to pay any amount to get what they wanted, then I suppose I would be out-voted by you and Ginny?"

"Yes, I suppose you would." Rich was being so cagey that I could only assume that he was feeling particularly stupid today, or else he was hiding something. "But don't worry," he grinned. "It would have to be a very good home with someone we know, before I'd agree. There is no point in rescuing a horse if we sell him off to any old home we know nothing about. Nevertheless, we could make a fairish profit, and money is always useful!"

We were turning onto Winterford Drove, the place where everyone gallops and all their horses know they do. Mr. Big began to plunge sideways, fighting for his head. Rich was laughing as they thundered away.

"You shouldn't let him win, you should make him walk!" I yelled after Rich, but he couldn't hear me. "Walk!" I roared at Tess, who was jogging and pulling to be off. She put in a couple of bucks, to signify her feelings of deprived martyrdom, then subsided to a mulish amble, her ears flat.

So that was it then. Rich had cleverly avoided the issue, but I was sure that Melissa must be 'the good home with someone we know' and Ginny, always a touch mercenary, although she called it practical, was busy bidding up the price to Mr. Hyde-Grant. Doubtless, I would hear all about it eventually, once Ginny had ensured us of the profit that they thought would stop me from being upset over losing

Tapestry. But I was upset. I would far rather have the horse than the money.

I was in a foul mood by the time I caught up with Rich. He was waiting for me at the end of Pikersfield Lane, still with the silly grin on his face, while Mr. Big steamed like a kettle beneath him.

"Oh very clever I'm sure, to get him all sweated-up like that! Now we'll have to walk for miles to dry him off," I said, coldly.

"You nag just like Ginny!"

"Don't you mention Ginny to me!" I shouldered Tess past the lathered chestnut and rode ahead, determined not to speak to Rich. He trotted Mr. Big up beside me.

"You really ought to have faith in your friends to do the right thing," he observed, blandly. I ignored him. Then he kept laughing to himself all the way home, as if he had a secret, which I knew he had anyway, and I could have throttled him. We rode under the clock arch into the yard, to be greeted by an incredible sight.

Tapestry was a horse with a strong constitution and a healthy appetite. He was still thin, but it had not taken him long to regain his interest in life and his handsome looks. He stood in the middle of the stable yard, his gray and white coat rippling multi-hued in the sunlight, just like the intricate patterns of a tapestry, after which he was named. His unusually dark black points, mane, and tail glowed their navy-blue highlights. He was wearing the antique, blue and gold sidesaddle.

The embroidered panels fell to below his belly line, the gold thread-work gleaming and winking in the light, while their gilt fringes and the tassels round the cushion-like seat, shimmered with his restless movement. Tapestry's long mane, combed to a silky fineness, cascaded to his shoulder, and his full tail swept the cobbles. He was wearing an old bridle that belonged to Mr. Big, but its cracked leather was sleeved in blue velvet, and the reins were scalloped with gold embroidered material. Melissa Anne Grant's horse stood before us, a living, breathing creature.

It took me a second or two to get over the shock, then "His mane is laid on the wrong side," was all I could think of to say.

"It has to be, don't you understand?" Melissa said, with that odd, fey expression in her eyes.

"I wanted to get at him with a pulling comb," Ginny admitted, "but Melissa wouldn't let me, and I'm glad now. It's uncanny how alike they look isn't it?"

"We made the bridle trimmings ourselves. We copied them exactly from the painting," Melissa said.

"No, I don't understand," I objected, crossly. Perhaps it was just because I was in a bad mood, but I could not see the point of the pantomime. "That saddle is extremely old and probably valuable. It will fall to pieces if you are not careful. Honestly, Melissa, you are not only being childish, but irresponsible. Your father will have 50 fits! Ginny, you should know better, instead of encouraging her."

"My, my, we did get out of bed the wrong side this morning, didn't we?" Ginny observed.

"Yes, I'd noticed that too," Rich agreed. He rode Mr. Big around Tapestry, for a better look. Tapestry arched his neck, danced on the spot and took a playful nip at Big's quarters as he passed. Sharing a paddock with Pearly had taught the big chestnut to be nimble on his feet, and he ducked smartly out of the way.

"Very dashing," Rich said, saving himself from departing via the side door by grabbing at Big's mane. "But the saddle looks a bit uncomfortable to me!"

"I would never ride on it," Melissa said. "I just needed to see what it looked like on Tapestry." She was being deliberately evasive and gave me no further explanation.

As far as I was concerned, it was all part of Melissa's rather unhealthy obsession with Melissa Anne Grant. She had come to identify herself with the girl in the painting to such a serious extent that she needed Tapestry Mark Two to look exactly like Tapestry Mark One. And she needed to own him.

Tapestry Mark Two progressed from stretching his legs with the other horses in the orchard, to being led round the lanes, and then to gentle exercise on the lunge. He was filling out, feeling his oats and ready for light work. I longed to ride him, but Tess' tack did not fit him and a new saddle and bridle were way beyond my means. I was furious when I returned, one morning, from helping Mom with the shopping, to see Rich riding Tapestry round the schooling area in the orchard. Melissa was sitting on the gate, looking pleased with herself.

"I bought Tapestry some new tack," she told me, smugly. "Daddy sent me a check."

He would, I thought.

"Rich asked the tack shop man to bring several saddles round in his van, so we could fit him properly, and Ginny chose a general purpose saddle with a spring tree and knee and thigh rolls."

More plotting, I thought.

"We have all tried it, and it's so comfortable."

So I'm the last one to ride Tapestry, after all, I thought.

"I chose a bridle with a stitched nose band, because it looks so smart, and Ginny decided that an eggbut snaffle bit would be best."

Don't bother to ask me what I think, I thought.

131

Rich walked Tapestry to the gate and dismounted. I had to admit that the tack, all dark, glowing, supple, top-quality leather, was exactly what I would have chosen, if I had been able to afford such luxuries. But it still rankled that none of them thought my opinion worth consulting, and I was willing to bet that, had I not turned up unexpectedly, no one would have bothered even to tell me.

"I didn't think you would be back so soon." Rich had the grace to look somewhat shame-faced, confirming my suspicion that the tack was meant to be a secret. "I've ridden him for only 10 minutes, so he's not at all tired, and he's absolutely terrific. I thought you'd like to try him out around the lanes this afternoon."

"How incredibly kind of you!" Rich did not appear to notice my sarcasm. "He is probably traffic-shy," I added, knowing full well that he was not. "And you should never have let Melissa ride him, he's far too big for her. When he's fit and in work, he will be far too much horse for her to manage." I was hoping to make a point here, but it seemed to go completely over Rich's head.

As it turned out, I was not able to ride Tapestry that afternoon. The sky turned ink black, rumbling with distant thunder, and we barely had time to stable the horses before a fearful storm hit Pikersfield. Torrential rain, driven before a gale force wind, lashed the buildings, while water swamped the yard and boiled down the drains. A premature dusk cloaked the Manor House in a gloom relieved only by sudden, livid lightning. At teatime, looking like a drowned rat, Mr. Hyde-Grant slammed in through the kitchen door.

Chapter Fourteen

The storm was still shaking the house when we gathered in Mr. Hyde-Grant's study that evening. My mother had lit the fire against the unexpected chill, and rain spat down the cavernous chimney to hiss onto the flaming logs. The wind hurled the downpour against the window in sharp, staccato blasts that rattled the lattice and thrashed the roses against the glass. The only light in the room was from the lamp on Mr. Hyde-Grant's desk, and from the flame that illuminated our tense, waiting faces. Rich and I sat on the sofa on one side of the arching, stone fireplace, Mom and Melissa on the sofa opposite, and Ginny squatted cross-legged on a rug in front of the hearth.

Spread in the pool of lamp light on the desk were the letters and scraps of parchment from Melissa Anne's room, each now encased in a protective, polyethylene sleeve, with a typed transcript beside it. Mr. Hyde-Grant was taking his time, setting them in order, and Melissa was too wound up to sit still. The wait, while her father put on dry clothes and had something to eat, had been almost too much for her to endure. By now, her nervous tension was affecting us all, and my mother was gripping Melissa's hand to still her fidgeting.

"It would be more fitting," Mr. Hyde-Grant began, "if I

told the tragic story of Melissa Anne Grant in that secret chamber that became her hiding place, almost her prison, for what was certainly the last year of her life. Sadly, that is not possible, but I hope, all the same, that she knows her story is being told.

"It would take far too long for me to read all the letters to you, so I will tell the story in my own words and quote the letters, here and there, to fill in the details.

"As you probably know, the reign of King Charles I of England was a time of political and religious crisis in this country. The King believed that he had a divine right to rule as he wished, but some people were beginning to question the King's prerogative, believing that Parliament should have more power. Charles had a Roman Catholic wife, Queen Henrietta Maria, Parliament was against what it called 'Popery,' the King tried to rule without Parliament, and the Parliamentarians whipped-up feelings against Roman Catholics, in order to cause religious agitation in the country that would turn the people against the King. It was to lead to the English Civil War.

"Melissa Anne and her brother, Thomas Charles Grant, grew up happily here in Somerset. They lived in a very fine mansion, that stood once where the Pikersfield Estate stands now. Their father had built the mansion in the days of his wealth, before the family circumstances were reduced by the persecution and fines suffered by Roman Catholics, and it had replaced the more humble Manor House on the estate as the family home. The Manor House was then rented to a Grant cousin who later became Melissa Anne's useless guardian. That manor House was, of course, this house – Pikersfield Manor, as is now known.

"When Melissa Anne was 12 years old, her parents took her and her brother, Thomas, to London, and the young people were presented at court. The family stayed in London for some years, and I believe that Melissa Anne became quite a favorite with Queen Henrietta Maria, who looked kindly on fellow Roman Catholics. That was when the portrait of Melissa Anne, that now hangs at the foot of the stairs, was painted by the court artist, Van Dyke.

"Unfortunately, by the year 1642 the trouble between the King and Parliament had become very serious. Melissa Anne and her mother returned to Somerset, thinking themselves safe enough on their remote country estate, but they were staunch Roman Catholics and Royalists. They were meant to be under the protection of the Grant cousin who lived in the nearby Manor House, but it seems he was something of a coward and hid himself away from the troubles. During the time that Parliament's power was growing and the Catholics were being persecuted for their faith, some of them made secret places in their homes where a priest could hide from unexpected visitors. That may have been the time when the little tunnel from the landing and the hidden chamber in the stable roof were constructed.

"According to the letters, Thomas Grant and his father did not return home with Melissa Anne and her mother, but stayed in London with a distant relative called Edward Hyde. Edward Hyde was an able lawyer who, by 1642, was favored and trusted by King Charles. The influence of his kinsman Hyde drew Thomas Grant very much into the center of events.

"There was no postal service, as we know it, in those days. Thomas had to send his letters to his family by the hands of messengers or traveling merchants, so they would have been few and far between, and sent only when he could be sure of their safe delivery. There were Parliamentary spies everywhere, seeking to intercept messages from the King's supporters, and Thomas would have to be careful no to endanger his sister and his mother by drawing attention to them.

"When King Charles fled to Nottingham in 1642, Thomas went with the court and found himself one of the small company of men in charge of the King's two sons, Charles, Prince of Wales, and young prince James. I will read you a piece from a letter that Thomas sent to his sister that year.

"'It was here in Nottingham, on the twenty-second day of August, that our King raised his standard in symbolic and ancient summons for his true subjects to come to his aid. Proud were we to rally to the King, and proud was I to have the two young Princes in my care. Prince Charles is in but his twelfth year and Prince James has seen but nine summers, yet they rode amongst the troops, brave Royalist Cavaliers all, and were much praised and cheered withal.'"

Mr. Hyde-Grant paused to sip from a glass of water. There was a deep silence in the room, broken only by the soughing of the wind in the chimney. Even Melissa had ceased to fidget. Her father picked up another letter.

"Those were brave early days for King Charles and his Cavaliers," he sighed. "The King's dashing cousin, Prince Rupert of the Rhine, led the cavalry, and you can feel the excitement in Thomas' next letter.

"'How certain were we of victory when we came to a place twixt Birmingham and Oxford, called Edgehill. It was the twenty-third day of October and a morning of frost, as I sat my horse atop the hill beside the young Princes and heard the crash of cannon and the ring of steel. Bravely Prince Rupert, in scarlet velvet and mounted upon his great, black Barbary horse, led the charge down upon Parliament's forces. But he thought not to leave a guard

136

upon the guns and standard of the King, and soon we were hard pressed. Notwithstanding his peril, the valiant Prince of Wales drew his pistol and cried that he feared them not. I laid hand upon his bridle and begged him spur for safety. Praise be to God that we rode thence unharmed and live to fight another day.'"

Mr. Hyde-Grant replaced the letter on his desk and shook his head sadly. "Poor Thomas, poor boy! They were to fight for so many more days and years! But you can see how devoted he was to the King and the young Princes. You must make allowances for him, and try to understand the sense of duty that kept him at his post rather than return home to protect his sister. Their parents died the next year, their father from battle wounds and their mother from a fever. Melissa Anne was left on her own, apart from the doubtful protection of her guardian cousin lurking here in his Manor House. She must have longed to hear from her brother, but it was nearly three years later, in 1645, when she received the next letter.

"'I am weary from this war and my heart is sore, dearest sister, for the peril in which you may be. We bide now in Bristol where Prince Charles, come to manhood now though but in his fifteenth year, commands the Royalist forces in the West. Our kinsman, Edward Hyde, gives advice and, I fear, seeks too much to rule the Prince, while in our confusion all goes not well with our cause. Be warned, beloved sister, the men of Parliament are become over bold, having those troops trained to fight with cursed efficiency by Oliver Cromwell. Plan for the contingency that you may need hide yourself from the Ironsides, your name being Grant, as is mine who am sought by them. Your guardian being but a broken reed, I fear for you, a maid alone in that great house save for servants, and some of them not to be trusted. Have faith in Edward Herbmaster always to serve our family with loyalty, but look not to Mistress Polly for sympathy, for I fear she is of the Puritan persuasion. I pray God there are others who we know not yet but will give you succor. I wish I could come to you, but I must with loyalty serve my Prince.'"

"But WHY?" Melissa burst out. "Why couldn't he go to her? How cruel of him! The Prince had whole armies to look after him and Melissa Anne was alone, his own sister and his closest living relative."

"Perhaps putting other things before family was a Grant character failing even then," Mr. Hyde-Grant said, grimly. "But worse was to come. This is what Thomas wrote 10 months later, in December 1645.

'Even as the King sends missives to his son, Prince Charles, urging him to escape, the armies of Parliament move west and we retreat before them. The defeat of the King at Nasby, on the thirteenth day of June this year, was a sorry one and I fear all is lost. With grief and fright did I receive your messenger, Edward Herbmaster, and from him hear that Cromwell's damned Ironsides had put our home to the torch. I thank God you were warned in time to escape. Well it was that our cousin contrived the secret chamber at the Manor House, but knowing that he, too, has taken to cowardly heels and fled, I pray his servants keep your secret close and care that you starve not. Being a Grant, it would go ill with you should you be taken, so show not yourself abroad until I send rescue.'

"It is a matter of record," Mr. Hyde-Grant said, consulting a note book, "that the Grant mansion was burnt down by a company of Cromwell's pikemen, who camped for some time on nearby common land. The area has been known as Pikersfield ever since. That was the last of

Thomas Grant's letters to his sister, and Melissa Anne Grant was never heard of again."

"Oh no!" Melissa leapt to her feet in agitation. "That can't be it. There has to be more!"

"Calm down, Melissa. I'm sorry, I shouldn't keep you in suspense. Have you forgotten the scraps of paper on the table? They were the hardest of all to read – and the most sad. Among them was this. I think it is a hastily scribbled note from Thomas to his sister, but it is unsigned and un-dated.

'I send this by the hand of one who has a fresher mount than I, whose horse has foundered. I am afoot and though but a few miles from you, struggle in the force of this fear-some storm. Prince Charles, our kinsman Hyde, and all their party are fled into Cornwall, thence to take ship to safety. I must surely follow, bearing such small funds as we have salvaged for the support of the Prince in exile. Have ready for me, I beg you, your good horse Tapestry, for I have need of his swift strength and can tarry with you but an instant, speed being of the essence. When my mission and my duty are done, I will return to bear you away to safety. Dear sister, wait for me.'"

"But he never came back, did he?" Melissa said, with a sob in her voice.

"Yes he did, but not for a very long time. Prince Charles and his followers sought refuge in Pendennis Castle, where Thomas caught up with them. On the second of March 1646 they sailed away from England, and I know for a fact that Edward Hyde and Thomas Grant were with the com-pany that shared the Prince's 14 years of exile in Europe. King Charles I was beheaded by Parliament in 1649 but, when Cromwell was dead and England weary of Puritan rule, Prince Charles was restored to the throne as King

Charles II. Thomas Grant and Edward Hyde returned to England with him in 1660, but by then, of course, Thomas was years too late to save his sister."

"You are taking a long time to get to the point, and it's upsetting Melissa," Ginny interrupted angrily.

"I'm sorry, but what happened to Thomas is all part of Melissa Anne's story. When the Prince came home to be King, he rewarded Edward Hyde for his loyalty by making him Earl of Clarendon and his chief minister. The King's younger brother, James, married Edward Hyde's daughter, and Thomas Grant married one of his Hyde cousins. Thomas became a very wealthy, well-connected young man and he changed his name to Hyde-Grant. This house has been in the family ever since, although Thomas never lived in it. Maybe he heard of the fate of his sister, so never came back here. It is certain that he did not disturb his sister's last hiding place, and he took its secret with him to the grave."

"Do you mean to tell us," Ginny shouted her fury, "that Melissa Anne's brother just pushed off abroad with the Prince, then came back when the Prince was made King, made his fortune, and married a sort of royal relation, and never cared what happened to his sister? Your family sure throws up some nasty characters every now and then!"

"Ginny, you are being very rude," my mother protested, but Mr. Hyde-Grant did not appear to take offense.

"Trust Ginny to cut through the waffle and get to the point," he chuckled. "That is a very neat summary and may even be true, but don't be so hard on Thomas! Perhaps he had no choice. Edward Hyde was a bit of a bossy character. Don't forget that Thomas said his kinsman tried to tell even the Prince what to do! I suspect that Edward Hyde ordered Thomas to go with them, or perhaps the horse, Tapestry,

foundered too, and Thomas had no other means of escape –
it was a long ride from Somerset into Cornwall, and
Thomas was pressed for time, so he must have ridden the
beast hard. We will never know the truth of the matter, but
I think I know what happened to Melissa Anne."

Ginny subsided back onto the hearth rug, looking unre-
pentant. Mr. Hyde-Grant picked up a plastic sleeve con-
taining one of the blackened scraps of parchment that had
lain for so long on Melissa Anne's table in the secret chamber.

"These are just random jottings, not a diary as I had
hoped, and there are no dates. Much of the writing even I
could not decipher. I think Melissa Anne was very ill when
she wrote the last part of it.

"Thomas sailed away with the Prince in March 1646 although, of course, Melissa Anne did not know that, and she
must have stayed here in hiding all the following summer,
expecting him to return any day. It seems that the servants
drifted away and the Manor House was looted and left
semi-derelict, but still she was determined to stay, knowing
that he would not know where else to look for her.

"She was devoted to that horse, Tapestry, and she men-
tions him often. He had been a present from her brother in
happier times, and losing him seems to have distressed her
every bit as much as her brother's failure to return. She
worried constantly that something had happened to
Tapestry. I think this was the last thing she wrote.

'The Autumn gales are come and I fear that I have the
ague. The water in the well is bad from the bodies of the
sheep that the soldiers cast down into it. I have no longer
the strength to search the hedgerows for berries and there is
naught left to eat or drink. Nightly I weep my great sorrow,
and wait and listen below for the sound of Tapestry's

hooves upon the road. I long to see my faithful horse again and, in seeing him, to know that Thomas is safe home.'"

Mr. Hyde-Grant put down the paper and folded his hands on his desk, with a finality that told us he had no more to say. We sat still and silent for a while. Even the wind had ceased to keen, as if holding its breath, waiting for the bitter end of the tale. Eventually, Melissa stirred and finished the story for us.

"She sobs, then her footsteps go but they don't come back. Melissa Anne must have died in the darkness of the stables below, listening hopelessly for hoof beats in the night. She was so weak and ill by then, that she did not have the strength to get back to her hiding place. But the room can't forget her. Her misery was so intense that it soaked forever into the place and we hear her still, weeping then walking down the stairs to watch for Tapestry and Thomas."

Without a doubt, Melissa had, yet again, divined the truth.

Chapter Fifteen

The storm blew itself out during the night. The next morning, everything looked fresh and sparkling under a bright sun, and Rich and Ginny were talking about going home. I heard the pound of feet and shouts of laughter as Rich, Ginny and Melissa thundered down the front stairs, something previously forbidden by Mr. Hyde-Grant's house-proud obsession. I heard Mr. Hyde-Grant's cheerful "good morning," called to them from his study, the door of which stood open onto the front hall, instead of closed against an intruding household, as once it had always been. My mother was singing in her bath. Everyone was happy – except for me.

I could not shake off the nagging sensation of a problem left unresolved, of a task only half done, of a duty – laid upon me, the minute I saw it, by the House of Tears – as yet unfulfilled. It had been Rich who asked Melissa how knowing the story of Melissa Anne would help, and his question had slipped past my consciousness unremarked. But now it recurred to me: we knew all there was to find out about the ghost of Pikersfield Manor, but what difference had it made? How had it helped Melissa Anne Grant?

It had helped the house and all those within its walls.

The atmosphere was altogether changed. The thralldom to the tears of the past was gone. Understanding, love, and laughter had lifted the gloom from the stone-flagged passageways, the paneled walls, the somber portraits, and the antique rooms. I was sure that Melissa Anne, her story told, had been forced to loose her hold on the place, to let it live again. She had been routed, chased in retreat to brood her sorrow alone in her own private place, never more to blight the lives of those who shared the same roof that had endured her time-haunting memory. Melissa Anne had gained nothing, in fact she was more alone now than ever before. I felt that I had let her down.

I expected Melissa, who had identified herself so closely with the sorrows of the sobbing ghost, to feel the same way but, obviously, she did not. Melissa was bubbling with happy excitement, as if she had not a care in the world and had forgotten all about Melissa Anne Grant. Because Melissa seemed cheerfully unaffected by the revelation of the sad history, Ginny could see no further need to worry about it either, and had dismissed the whole episode from her mind, except to complain that Mr. Hyde-Grant's telling of it had involved far too many dates. As long as one knew what had happened, Ginny declared, it really didn't matter when it happened. Rich tried to argue with her but gave up. Ginny bounced round the kitchen, looking mysterious.

"I'm going to cook mountains of bacon and eggs," she told me, "then I want everyone to have breakfast together. I've got a surprise for you, Anna, or rather, Mr. H-G has!"

"Here it comes," I thought. Judging by their faces, as they tackled the heaped plates Ginny set before them, everyone knew what Ginny meant and I was the only one in the dark. Mom looked flushed with pleased excitement, and she kept glancing at Melissa in a conspiratorial manner. Rich was laughing to himself again, and Mr. Hyde-Grant was hiding something under the table.

"Well, get on with it, Mr. H-G!" Ginny prompted. He stood up, hiding whatever it was behind his back.

"Ladies and gentleman," he began. Melissa giggled. "And Anna in particular. I have to announce that I have made a very important purchase. I have bought Tapestry."

"You would have been out-voted anyway," Ginny interrupted as she looked at me. "We own Tapestry too, so it was two to one!"

"If you would kindly let me finish!" Mr. Hyde-Grant glared at Ginny. "I have bought Tapestry for you, Anna. Well, the other two thirds of him, to be strictly accurate." With a flourish, he produced the new bridle with the stitched noseband from behind his back. "I couldn't gift-wrap the horse, so his bridle will have to do as a token."

"That's because he comes complete with tack," Melissa said. She was positively glowing with her delight in being able to give me such a present. "The tack was meant to be a surprise as well, but you came home early and caught us at it. And he has rugs for the winter, and absolutely everything else he will need, right down to the last brush, bucket, and tail bandage. It's all hidden in one of the empty stables."

I was opening and shutting my mouth like a fish out of water. I must have looked ridiculous.

"I told you to trust your friends to do what was right," Rich grinned, "but you were having such a wonderful time feeling sorry for yourself, that I thought we should let you enjoy wallowing in it for a while!"

"You rotten beast," I croaked. "But Mr. Hyde-Grant, I, well, I can't tell you how grateful…" He held up his hand to silence me.

145

"I told you I owed you a debt of gratitude. Tapestry is merely a very small part of the repayment. I owe you all a debt of gratitude." Mr. Hyde-Grant glanced round the table, "I'm going to miss you, Ginny and Rich, and I'm sure Melissa will, too. A big house like this needs to be full of cheerful young people, so come to see us often. There will always be beds for you here, and stables for your horses, any time you like."

"Thanks, Mr. H-G, we'll take you up on that." Ginny pushed back her chair. "But now we really must get going. Anna, do shut your mouth before you swallow a fly!"

"You didn't really think we would sell Tapestry to anyone else, did you?" Rich asked me, looking hurt.

"I thought Melissa wanted him," I admitted. Melissa squealed with amusement.

"He's far too big for me, any idiot can see that!" she laughed. "I'd far rather ride Tess. You will agree to loaning me Tess, won't you, Anna? I'd rather counted on it, but I couldn't ask first, without giving away the secret. Dad says he will pay for her shoes and keep and everything."

Still feeling faint from surprise and relief, I assured Melissa that nothing would please me more than to loan Tess to such a good home. I did not tell her that it was what I had planned from the start.

Melissa and I decided to ride part of the way back to Swallowbridge with Ginny and Rich. I ran a brush over the dapple-gray coat of *my* beautiful horse, saddled him with *my* fine new saddle, and glanced round the palatial stables that were, now, Tapestry's and Tess' permanent home. Life seemed almost too perfect to be true.

For a nasty moment it had occurred to me that, because Melissa no longer needed a nurse, Mom might be out of a job and we would have to leave Pikersfield Manor. Mr.

Hyde-Grant refused to hear of such a thing. He was, he said, a busy man with work that must continue to keep him away from home a lot of the time. He would always need a housekeeper to take care of the house, and to be a mother to Melissa.

"That makes us more or less sisters!" Melissa said happily. It might, I thought, take me a while to get used to that idea.

Tapestry strode out down the lane, his ears pricked with the pleasure of being out and about again. I gloried in his long, level stride and the feeling of power under my saddle, not to mention the fact that I no longer had to cramp my legs into shortened leathers, pretending that my mount was not too small for me. Melissa jogged beside me on Tess, chattering like a magpie.

"I can't wait to go to a gymkhana, as soon as I can ride well enough. Do you think I'll be ready before the end of the summer holidays, Ginny? Can I come to watch you and Rich at Chawton Show next week? And you will come to stay again soon, won't you? We'll have to go to the next horse sale, because Dad says I can rescue a pony because we'll have far too much grass now that shepherd has taken his sheep away, and something will have to eat it. If we all went fruit picking, we could rescue two ponies and start a retirement home."

"You do realize that there are only 24 hours in a day?" Rich asked dryly, when Melissa paused for breath.

"And before you do anything else, Melissa," Ginny pointed out, "you will have to learn to canter without falling off!"

"That was below the belt," I objected.

"I don't mind," Melissa grinned. "I deserved it."

It was only then that I realized how much Melissa had

changed. I felt that I could claim some of the credit for myself, but I knew that Melissa's metamorphosis from disturbed misery into this normal, happy, chattering child
was, in the main, thanks to Melissa Anne Grant. Thinking
about the sad spirit, un-helped and un-thanked, cast a shadow ahead of me, as we rode on into the green and gold,
summer-bright morning.

That shadow stayed with me, to make the rest of the week,
after the departure of Ginny and Rich, seem even more of
an anticlimax. Melissa and I rode every day. Mrs. Poppy
sang out of tune above the hum of her hoover. Mom talked
Mr. Poppy into taking on a lad to help him tidy up the garden. Mr. Hyde-Grant returned to Oxford and Melissa was
quite happy about his going. She felt, now, emotionally se-
cure enough to accept that her father had his work to do,
and to trust his promise to come home every weekend.

The most convincing evidence of Melissa's recovery
was her bedroom. I came across her trundling her monster
television set along the landing to the housekeeper's apartment, and I discovered most of her possessions heaped
round my room. She was, she said, going to share with me
while her own room was redecorated. She could not think
how she had managed to put up for so long with those awful, clashing colors, and her father was sure that a stone-
mason could sand the aerosol paint from the fireplace. I
was touched that, in a house that boasted half a dozen spare
bedrooms, Melissa would rather share mine. She had not,
of course, thought to ask me if I minded – complete mira-
cles don't happen over night!

But then I remembered the intense pleasure Melissa had
shown in the connivance of her father's secret purchase for
me of Tapestry. I guessed that she coveted the horse for

herself, and I knew that her keeping of the secret meant that she could not be sure, beforehand, that she would have the loan of Tess instead. Her only thought had been to make me happy. As a sister, real or unofficial, Melissa Hyde-Grant had to be one of the best.

Later that evening, I discovered that Melissa had vanished. I searched the house, but there was no sign of her. I did not want to pass on the worry to my Mother – old habits die hard – and I had become used to taking responsibility for Melissa and her strange behavior. I knew she had not gone wandering to look for the cats, because they were heaped in front of the stove, fast asleep. It was unlikely that she had gone out to see the horses, because we had already hung the late night hay nets. Nevertheless, outside was the only place that she could be.

The stable yard was in darkness but not silent. I could hear a horse shifting restlessly in its straw, and then Tess' sharp whinny. Her black and white face was peering over her stable door, and her head turned to look anxiously up and down the walkway. I went to see what was disturbing her, and quickly discovered the reason for her unease. Tapestry was not in his box next door.

Surely Melissa was not silly enough to go riding at night on her own? A check of the tack room told me that she had not, because Tapestry's tack was still on its rack and his head collar still on its hook. Maybe she had turned him out but, no, the orchard was empty. I dithered, worrying, in the yard, unsure what to do next. Only then did I notice a faint glow behind the windows of the old stable block.

I crossed the yard, pushed open the door and stepped three hundred years back in time. An antique horn lantern hung from a beam, to cast its soft light along the row of wooden partitions and the dusty, cobbled floor. In the end stall, his towering presence seeming to fill the small space, stood Tapestry. He was backed into the stall, and held there by pillar reins from his bit to the old iron rings on either side, put there centuries ago for just such a purpose. He was wearing the blue velvet sidesaddle and antique accoutred bridle. Just so would the groom have left the Tapestry of old, ready and waiting for his owner, Melissa Anne Grant, to come for him.

Tapestry saw me. He tossed his head against the pillar reins, so that his long mane rippled in the lantern light, then struck out in front of him with an impatient hoof. The embroidered saddle panels swung against his sides, and flashed rich gold and blue. The strike of his steel shoe was loud on the cobbles.

"Shush, don't upset him!" Melissa was crouched in a stall further down the building. She beckoned to me to join her.

"What are you doing?" I asked.

"I'm not exactly sure, although it's an idea that has been growing in my mind, ever since I heard that the old Tapestry and your gray horse looked so much alike. It's a long shot, but it might work. I had to do something. I should have told you, but you were so cross, the last time I put the side-saddle on Tapestry, that I thought you'd try to stop me."

Melissa reached up and unhooked the lantern, setting it down at our feet. Tapestry's stall, at the far end of the building, next to the hidden tack room, was now in shadow. I noticed that the tack room door was wedged open.

"Can't you leave her in peace?" I protested.

"That's just the point. When my father gets busy next week, she will have no peace. Surely you've noticed, the sobbing voice is heard only when something that belonged to Melissa Anne is disturbed? When you found the tack

150

room and touched her saddle, she cried. When we were all in her secret chamber that night, we heard her again. My great, great, grandfather knew it too, that was why he blocked off the old tack room and stopped using the stables."

"So we should do the same," I said.

"Impossible," Melissa sighed. "Dad has to empty the priest's hole, and I can understand why. There is no way he will agree to leave all those valuable things up there to rot. He has a team of students coming down from Oxford next week to catalogue everything and take it away. There will be bright lights, milling people, tramping feet, and everything disturbed. Dad is worried about having to do it, and he promised me that he will shut the room up for good when it is all done, but can you imagine what effect it will have on Melissa Anne?"

I could very well imagine, and it did not bear thinking about.

"I have talked it over with Mr. Poppy," Melissa continued. "He's a wonderful old man, and I feel awful about how rude I've always been to him! He knows so many extraordinary things and he has helped me a lot. He found the old lantern, and showed me how to use the pillar reins, and he told me all he could remember about the legend of the Wailing Woman. I'm sure that now is the moment when time has come full circle, and everything is in place to bring an end to the tears. I am kin, the same family, the same name even, so I have to do it."

I could see what Melissa meant. The cast was assembled: Melissa Anne's blood relation, Tapestry come home again, the help *un-looked for* from sympathetic strangers, the herb-master always loyal to the family, even the disapproving servant with puritan tendencies. All were gathered once more at the old Manor House in an uncanny coinci-

151

dence that had turned back the clock. But still I was doubt-ful. "I don't see how bringing Tapestry in here can help. It is her brother she cries for. You can't conjure Thomas Grant out of thin air, even with a look-alike horse."

"Remember the last thing she wrote?" Melissa quoted softly, "'I long to see my faithful horse again, and in seeing him to know that Thomas is safe home.' As soon as I heard that, I knew what I had to do and could stop worrying about her. Otherwise, there would have been no point in the finding out, would there?"

I knew, now, why Melissa had not been burdened with the same sense of failure that had overshadowed me since the telling of Melissa Anne's story. Instinctively, Melissa had been laying her plans from the onset, and all she had lacked was the guidance from Melissa Anne's own words, to show her how to carry them out. Now, there was nothing else to do but wait.

So, together and in silence, we waited as the long min-utes ticked towards the time when the ghost usually cried from being disturbed. Tapestry's head drooped and he dozed. The candle in the horn lantern spluttered and smoked. The air felt as thick and heavy as the drifting dust of the passing centuries, that muffled the beams and grayed the ancient stone walls. I leaned back against the partition, my eye-lids heavy.

We heard no sobbing. Perhaps the secret chamber was too far away and too thickly lined with boards for the sound to reach us. It was Tapestry's sudden restlessness that roused us. He had moved forwards, as far as the pillar reins would allow, his neck arched against the bit, his ears flick-ing nervously and his shifting feet stamping the cobbles.

Melissa and I shuffled forwards, and looked round the end of the partition towards the tack room door. At first there was nothing to see, except for Tapestry's tossing head and plunging forelegs. Then, drifting towards us came the haunting fragrance of lavender, that intensified until the air was heady with the scent of it, and something moved in the doorway.

The figure was unsubstantial, as if formed of shifting shadows, and of memories almost made flesh and left etched on time by the impact of so much emotion. But it was, unmistakably, Melissa Anne Grant. Her fair hair tumbled to her shoulders, fine lace at her neck, and wrists glimmered in the lantern light and her dark blue velvet skirts swept the floor. Her face was turned towards the horse, and the lovely eyes radiated joy. Slowly, she raised her hand and laid it on Tapestry's neck.

Tapestry gave a ringing cry, whether from fear or in greeting I could not tell. Mingled with the sound were the echoes of a girl's laughter. The phantom figure began to fade, sucking away with it the happy voice and the last traces of lavender flower perfume, until Melissa Anne Grant was gone.

"So that is the end of the story of the Wailing Woman of Pikersfield!" Melissa said, in a matter of fact tone. She jumped to her feet and shook the dust from her jeans. "This time she didn't walk down the building to look for Thomas, she simply faded away. She will rest in peace now and never come back."

Truly, the circle was complete. The two Melissas and the two tall, gray horses had shared a moment removed from the natural sequence of time, to touch each other briefly and pass across the centuries the good news of Thomas Grant's safe return. The haunting of the House of Tears was at an end.